The Chosen Ones

Oglala Warriors

A Series of Campfire Story Telling

The Chosen Ones
Oglala Warriors

A Series of Campfire Story Telling

JERRY BARRETT

www.jerrybarrett.net

Copyright (c) 2020 Jerry Barrett

All Rights Reserved

Printed in the United States of America

ISBN 978-1-7349377-0-1

Dedication

I dedicate this series of novels "The Chosen Ones Oglala Warriors" to the welfare of the Oglala Lakota Indians and all other Indigenous American people and most especially the youthful. My goal is to bring awareness of the Oglala Lakota people and their plight and need for assistance. Any help given is not charity, but simply a repayment of a debt we owe all indigenous people in our beloved country, for giving up their homes and way of life. Our strength as a nation is in our brotherhood to all citizens and love for our God. Most of all I dedicate all my creative abilities to my God. Without Him and His gift of love, I am lost. I am truly blessed by His love.

Tatanka Ska Son

Introduction of

The Chosen Ones Oglala Warriors:

The "Chosen Ones" is the story of the lives of three young Oglala Lakota Indians who live in the early 18th century in present day South Dakota. The three friends are blood brothers and are dedicated to each other throughout their entire lives. They are visited by the Son of God, in the form of a white buffalo and are blessed by Him with special powers and gifts of varied talents. They are chosen to be campfire story tellers to teach others of Wakantanka (God) and His Son, Tatanka Ska Son (Jesus) in the form of a white buffalo, known to many as being wakan (holy).

This is the first book in a series of novels "The Chosen Ones Oglala Warriors" and is a compilation of the adventures of three Oglala Lakota Indian braves and their encounters with Tatanka Ska Son and other Indian tribes in their many missions throughout the western states of this early American era. Join in on the campfire story telling adventures. Who knows you may be a campfire story teller soon after reading about those who are. In the meantime, sit down by our campfire and read about "The Chosen Ones Oglala Warriors" and enjoy the warmth of adventure.

Lakota Chief Sitting Bull

Contents

Acknowledgment 2

Preface 3

1. Bear Attack and New Brother 7

2. The Hunt of the Bull Moose 19

3. Mato Hota Takes a Prisoner 29

4. A Great Bear Chase 45

5. Fishing, Bears and Wolves 57

6. The Earlier Earth and Mother Earth 73

7. A Young Woman's Dance and a Brave Rescue 89

8. Man of the Sun 105

9. Sun Man's Rescue Sends a Strong Message 121

10. The Great Battle on the High Cliff Edge 133

Appendix 149

ACKNOWLEDGMENTS

This is a work of fiction. This book is the first in a series of novels about <u>The Chosen Ones Oglala Warriors</u>, involving three main characters, of the Oglala Lakota Indian people. All of the characters, organizations, and events portrayed in this novel are either products of this author's imagination and/or used fictitiously.

I would like to thank most of all my wife for assistance in editing, her support of my work and for being my soul mate.

Many thanks go to Robert Seckman for his help in strengthening my knowledge of the Pine Ridge Reservation and some of the problems existing there. He has been a benefactor for the Oglala Lakota for years. He has also helped with editing.

A huge thank you goes to Doris Seckman for her unselfish effort in editing of this first novel. I am most grateful for her support and encouragement.

I want to thank both Robert and Doris for their boundless support and friendship, it means the world to me.

Others I thank for their editing and input are:

Tami A. Strosahl, my dear friend, for her technical support in creating the website and help with editing.

Thank you to my brother, Preston, for introducing me to Wanda Collins, whose hard work and perseverance made this book possible, by her years of experience in publishing, graphics and engraving. She, also, has a keen eye for editing.

Some BING artwork was used in this book.

Preface

The Chosen Ones Oglala Warriors

In the early 1980's this author became aware of some of the plights of the Oglala Lakota Indian people of the Pine Ridge Indian Reservation. Over the years since those earlier times, the plight of the Oglala Lakota Indians has moved my concerns for the welfare of the Oglala Lakota children to have hope and a faith in one who loves them.

Many of the children are abused, by the results of drug and alcohol overuse by parents, who suffer from lack of hope, primarily because of eighty-five percent unemployment among those on the reservation. This is a sad state of affairs and the citizens of this great country should direct more resources and attention to solving the problems of these fine people who lost their lands and culture to the pioneers who came long ago to take lands and resources for their own. They destroyed the hunting grounds, took the lands from the Indians, shut down their culture and ways of living in the arms of Mother Earth and following the customs of their forefathers, and used force to subjugate them to their religious beliefs. To believe in God is a choice of each individual, as stated in our Constitution. We did not give the American Indian these rights and these rights were stolen from them and caused great damage to their culture, freedom to worship and live as they please in the pursuit of happiness.

Their ancestral heritage was stolen, by the wašicun (white man). This is not a statement of fiction but a fact documented by our country's historical records. We, the American people, must honor our debt which we all owe to all indigenous American Indians.

Any help or assistance to better their living conditions, educational and career opportunities and social acceptance, is sorely needed at this time in our history as a country which was founded on "In God We Trust". This assistance should stand at the forefront of our charitable giving. We as good servants to humanity on a whole give billions of dollars in aid to foreign countries and that has been honorable. However, we should put our own people first, when they are taken care of, then any excess funds or other types of aid can go to those in need worldwide.

The purpose of this book series is to raise awareness of the American Indians and their needs, and to let them know there are those who may not be physical members of their tribe, but are tribal members in mind, spirit and heart. This author has chosen the Oglala Lakota people as his people to support.

This series is about the lives of three Oglala Lakota Indians as they grow up and their special relationship with Tatanka Ska Son (Jesus in the form of a white buffalo). This book series has many adventures and teaches some Oglala Lakota language and other dialects. The entire language and dialect meaning section for "The Chosen Ones Oglala Warriors" is listed in alphabetical order in the Appendix back of the book.

This book series is for anyone who loves adventure and the American Indian culture, along with learning about honor, respect and character-building traits through Campfire Story Telling. Thank you for your support. Keep the campfires burning, and may Wakantanka (God) Bless You.

Jerry Barrett

Tipi

Lakota Warrior

Chapter 1

Bear Attack and New Brother

The great red sun which lights and warms Mother Earth has drifted behind the mountains in the western lands of the Oglala (to scatter one's own) Lakota (the Siouan people) Indians. A cold breeze is whispering across a mountain stream and gently fans the campfire of three young Oglala Lakota Indian boys Mato Hota (a grizzly bear - Lakota dialect), who is the unofficial leader of the trio and the son of the chief of their village. He is taller than his two friends, stocky with broad shoulders and strong for his years, as puberty has been working to build him into a powerful brave and perhaps chief someday. Luzahan (swift – Lakota dialect), is almost as tall as Mato Ḣota, but thin and wiry, with strong long muscles and can out run anyone in the village his age. He is the quieter of the boys, with a more serious manner about him as a normal youth. He is loyal and brave and a good friend to his Indian brothers. Ciqala (little one – Lakota dialect), is short in stature, with broad shoulders and thick body build, with large strong calves and very strong for his size. He is always looking for fun and is the talkative of the three young Indians; he is very loyal and is a valuable friend to Mato Ḣota and Luzahan. All three Oglala Lakota boys are soon coming of age to be recognized as braves among their tribe.

The three young Indian boys are huddled close to their campfire laughing at a story Mato Ḣota is telling about an old  capa (beaver), who came upon a big šungmanitu (a wolf) trying to break into his neighbor's capa lodge. Mato Ḣota, half laughing continues his story, "That old capa just swam out of his lodge and saw this big gray šungmanitu, biting and tearing at the twigs on top of the beaver lodge nearest to shore, using his strong jaws, sharp teeth and big front paws trying to get in to eat his good neighbor. Old capa quietly ducked underwater and swam over behind the big gray šungmanitu. He came up fast from underwater and bit that big bad šungmanitu right in the tail end. Off went that big bad šungmanitu howling, yapping and screaming in pain, never to return again to this place of the quiet creek."

All three Oglala Lakota boys were laughing wildly now. As they started to become quiet again, Mato Ḣota could hardly keep

Bear Attack and New Brother

from bursting out laughing, but settles down and becomes serious in his manner and slowly asks, "You know what else"? Luzahan and Ciqala look at Mato Hota with great interest. Mato Hota slowly continues, "That big bad šungmanitu didn't know, that old capa only had one big tooth." Now, they all roll around on the ground laughing uncontrollably, slapping each other in fun. It is a good day to be a young Oglala Lakota Indian gathered around a warm campfire, exchanging stories among Mother Earth's wonders.

Little do they know that a great big golden mato hota (a grizzly bear) has heard their noisy laughter and is silently closing  the distance through the tall trees toward their campsite. The huge golden colored mato hota has stopped about one hundred feet from the campfire and is watching the boys through his evil black eyes, as darkness sets in on the three young Oglala Lakota Indians, who are completely unaware of his presence and the danger coming their way, at any moment.

Young Mato Hota says to Luzahan and Ciqala, "We better get in our blankets and be ready for an early hunt. If we can kill the giant moose and harvest his meat, we will be in good standing with our chief and stand tall with the other braves and have good favor with all in our village." Ciqala replies, "Good fireside council Mato Hota, I am tired laughing, my belly hurts from your story telling. Rest well in your blanket my brother." The three settle down in their multi-colored woven blankets, made for them by their good mothers. Sleep soon overtakes them as the swift mountain stream and night creatures sing out for company or just plain happiness and contentedness.

The big golden colored mato hota is slowly creeping towards the three sleeping Oglala Lakota boys on his gigantic paws. One at a time, they move closer, showing long claws visible by moon light breaking through the trees. Having reached about fifty feet from the sleeping boys the big mato hota begins charging through the surrounding bush growling ferociously, as he charges the unsuspecting sleeping Oglala Lakota boys.

Young Mato Hota is the first to react and grabs his spear and throws it with all his might, hitting and wounding the big golden mato hota in the shoulder, but his charge is not stopped, only slowed, as he bites the spear and pulls it from his left shoulder with his powerful jaws, biting it in two. The great grizzly bear is even more enraged by his new pain inflicted by Mato Hota's spear wound deep in his shoulder. Mato Hota —with the same name as the one charging in on him— is frozen in place. The great mato hota's full attention is totally focused on this young Oglala Lakota Indian as he charges directly toward him, ignoring the other terrified defenseless companions completely.

The huge mato hota is within twenty feet of the young brave, when suddenly out of the night's clear sky, streaks a blue beam of light and it lands between the charging ferocious mato hota and the terrified young Indian boys. The great golden grizzly slides to a halt before the beam of blue light, which begins to slowly reveal Tatanka Ska Son, Son of Wakantanka, God, the Creator (appearing as a tatanka ska, white buffalo), now standing facing the giant golden mato hota. It is a young huge tatanka ska, the young Oglala Lakota boys see appearing out of the blue beam of light.

The blue beam is now showing his huge size in full splendor, glistening with pure long white fur, hanging down his broad shoulders and down his front legs. His head is massive, with long

Bear Attack and New Brother

smooth black horns protruding from each side of his massive white fur covered head and are shining brightly with the light from the blue light beam that surrounds him.

The huge golden mato hota looks straight at the White Buffalo Spirit's big blue eyes, swings around swiftly and bolts, crashing headlong through the heavy brush and disappears into the deep woods, never to return again to this place. He heads as swiftly as he can go over many mountains far away from the Oglala Lakota people, as Tatanka Ska Son had planned for him to do all along.

Luzahan and Ciqala are now standing beside their brother, young Mato Hota. The soon to be young braves are completely spellbound, frozen in place with fear and amazement. Tatanka Ska Son, wheels around on His big black cloven front hooves, facing the three amazed Indian youths, who are standing spell bound in place, wearing fearful looks upon their faces. Tatanka Ska Son speaks, "Do not fear Me; I have come to be your takolaku (his special friend). I will be a friend and brother to you three chosen ones from now until I return to be with My Father, Wakantanka in Mahpiya (Heaven). I am sent by My Father, Wakantanka, as you see. I come in the form of a tatanka ska (of which most Indian tribes have knowledge of as sacred) and not as an image of My Father, Wakantanka.

"I have come to tell the story of the words of My Wakan (Holy) Father, The Great Spirit, the Creator, God. He who awaits all wicaša (man, a man, mankind), who love and believe in Him and I, His Son, Tatanka Ska Son, as known to your people, as Mahpiya.

"Those who listen and choose to believe My story will join Wakantanka and Me in Mahpiya, far into the stars above the mountains high. I am here to teach all tribes, bands and people of this earth, about My Father. For those who believe in My Father and I, many will be building their tipi fires in Mahpiya, which will never burn cold, that is His solemn promise.

"As for you three, I am to be called, Tatanka Ska Son. I come to you and all others in the form of a tatanka ska, that all who believe the white buffalo is wakan (holy) will understand who I am among all Indian people," said the Son of Wakantanka (God). The three young braves drop to their knees and cross their arms across their chests. Mato Hota speaks up in a humble tone, "My Tatanka Ska Son, what can we do to please You, Oh Great One"?

Tatanka Ska Son answers, "I am to be called Tatanka Ska Son, little Oglala Lakota called Mato Hota. I have chosen you three young Oglala Lakota, as My closest friends and brothers here on Mother Earth. My Father, Wakantanka, has chosen to favor your Oglala Lakota tribe above all others on this earth, and your tribe will be My tribe and I will camp in your land as long as many moons have shown among the stars.

"These are My Words just as I, Tatanka Ska Son, have spoken them. I come to help the Oglala Lakota people and spread many words in stories to be told and handed down by many campfires, to save all people who believe in Wakantanka and His Son, who stands before you in this place."

Tatanka Ska Son continues speaking to all three young Oglala Lakota, "Mato Hota told a funny story and all laughed and gave the funny story little more thought, now I will teach you to look at the wise and lasting life lesson to be found within

Bear Attack and New Brother

it, to be remembered and kept deep inside your spirit for all time and passed down to all, by the campfires of many moons to come among your people.

"In Mato Hota's story, the old capa was no match in fighting strength with that of the big gray šungmanitu, but his strength and bravery, dwelled in his love for his fellow brother's life. Old capa was willing to give his life to protect his brother capa. Old capa knew he was weak with many waniyetus (winters) age and only had one tooth to use as a weapon, but he was brave and wise. He knew he could stalk the šungmanitu under water and surprise him from behind and use his one tooth bite in the tail to warn him away from his evil plan against his colony of capa brothers. He was ready to give his life for a friend. Each one of you are brothers and should always put your brother's lives before your own, for it is love that binds you as brothers.

"One day I will show you this great love, and that is the real lesson to be found in Mato Hota's funny story. It is My Wish, that you will all tell this story for fun among your people, as young Mato Hota has told it and then tell it as I have told you, for all to hear and carry forward My Words. This story is a lesson in life's journey on Mother Earth in the customs and honorable way of the Oglala Lakota. Sleep now, for when the light breaks over the mountain, We will go and find the big moose you seek to feed your tribe, now My brothers, come close to the fire and sleep My new 'Story Tellers', it is time."

Mato Hota can hardly believe he is not dreaming of being in Mahpiya, at this very moment, as he looks from his warm blanket at the big mound of white fur lying between the young Oglala Lakotas, their campfire and the dark woods filled with many unknown dangers. He looks at Luzahan who is staring at him and then Ciqala and then toward the sleeping Tatanka Ska Son. Mato Ḣota signals to Ciqala to go to sleep.

Morning finds Tatanka Ska Son drinking water from the cold clear mountain stream which has been singing her beautiful sounds of peacefulness all through the night. Complete harmony has filled the hearts of the young soon to be great 'Story Tellers'. Tatanka Ska Son walks back to the camp fire, which He has kept burning all night, without moving from His prone position near the young Oglala Lakota boys. The three have noticed this rare warm fire greeting in the early morning and look at each other in total amazement. Mato Ḣota speaks up to his brothers, "Who kept the campfire going all night"? Luzahan and Ciqala each shake their heads in denial and then all three peer in the direction of Tatanka Ska Son, who says softly in a deep Voice befitting His great size and strength, "It was a small comfort I could provide for My new 'Story Tellers', cold hurts to the bone. Put out the fire now and let Us go find the big moose you are trying to hunt, the very one My Father has provided for the Oglala Lakota upon His Mother Earth."

The three climbed upon the prone massive back of Tatanka Ska Son, ready for new adventure. Tatanka Ska Son warns, "Hold on tight My little brothers, you ride with the wind." With the three young braves hanging on for dear life, each with hands full of the white fur of Tatanka Ska Son, He lofts off and flies, skimming along near the surface of the rushing water rapids of the cold mountain stream in what seems like slow motion to the

three young Oglala Lakota. Each young brave is having the time of their short lives, now surely living in an earthly Mahpiya, riding aboard the back of Tatanka Ska Son, the Son of Wakantanka (God, the

Bear Attack and New Brother

Creator). Soon they fly over the area where the bull moose is feeding and Mato Hota spots his exact location and puts it to his memory.

Tatanka Ska Son's deep Voice bellows loudly in excitement, "Now that you have seen the big moose, let Us fly among the eagles, high in the mountains My brothers." He makes a sharp move, flying upward toward the nearby mountain range and Mato Hota riding on Tatanka Ska Son's neck yells back at Luzahan and Ciqala, "Hold on, be brave my brothers."

As the four reached high above into the cold mountain air, an eagle flies up near to Tatanka Ska Son's head. Tatanka Ska Son spoke unknown words, numerous times to the eagle and the eagle screeched back, as if to answer and then peeled off and flew swiftly away, flapping his big wings, with strong even strokes. It seemed to Mato Hota, that it was as if the great eagle was given a command or mission to carry out by Tatanka Ska Son.

Very soon one by one, eagles began joining the big Tatanka Ska Son, and His young Oglala Lakota companions, as They flew in and out through the clouds high, then low among and between the mountains, with an occasional dive into narrow mountain passes, that was very scary for them, but very exciting fun for the young Oglala Lakota boys to be living this day, in this way, with this new loving Master.

Think about this, can anyone imagine seeing hundreds of eagles, a white buffalo with three Indian boys on His big back, All flying in formation, high in the mountains? What a sight that must have been to a young Indian brave from the Crow (Apsáalooke – children of the large-beaked bird – Siouan language) tribe, who lived over the mountains from the Lakota

People of the Oglala band. He was startled while hunting a big sintesapela (black-tail or mule deer) and was just about to shoot his arrow at it, when it was spooked causing it to jump high, as if it were shot, and then it ran swiftly away through the deep woods.

Arikara (running wolf – Crow dialect) stood motionless and watched in total amazement as the strange squadron of nature, flew directly overhead. When They had passed overhead and moved off slowly in the distant mountains and disappeared straight into the sun, he bolted, running toward his village, dodging through the trees at a full run, occasionally stumbling and falling down while running so fast he could not keep his feet under him, straight toward his village home.

When Arikara reached his village, he was breathless and he hurriedly entered the lodge of his mother and told her what he had seen. She did not believe him and sternly told him, to tell no one of this strange story, or they would think of him as Crazy Wolf, not Running Wolf. He would listen to his wise mother and stay silent about what he saw, but still he could not put what he saw out of his mind, for he had truly seen what he told his mother about, it was no dream, it was real.

Meanwhile, Tatanka Ska Son had returned Mato Hota and his Oglala Lakota brothers to their night camp. Landing softly near the cold campfire within a circle of stones, the young braves had made from the mountain stream next to camp. Tatanka Ska Son speaks, "I leave you here, so you may begin your hunt of the big bull moose."

The young Oglala Lakotas climbed down from their huge furry perch and stood in amazement, starring at their new Brother and Friend, who is filled with unknown powers. Mato

Bear Attack and New Brother

Hota dares to speak most respectfully, "Oh Great One, Tatanka Ska Son, we are most honored by Your calling us brother, and to ride among the great eagles high in the mountain air, as no other has done. It will be a story to pass on to all. We are most grateful."

Tatanka Ska Son replies, "Today, our flight among the mountains and through the clouds was My way for you to see some of Mother Earth through My eyes and begin to understand My Father's greatness and to see Mother Earth, whom He loves as the Creator of all, that is or will ever be, from His eyes. I serve Him here, as your Brother, Teacher and speak Words of His Will for all to follow."

Mato Hota speaks up again, "My Great Brother, Tatanka Ska Son; may I ask for Your help in today's hunt of the big moose downstream"? Tatanka Ska Son replies, "I have already helped you My brother, by giving you the skill to hunt and the will to become great braves among your tribe. If I help each one of you in the hunt of the big moose, there would be no honor for you to share together and receive from your tribal family. If I provide the big moose as a gift to them, the honor would be Mine, not yours. Can you see wisdom in these My Words, My little brother, Mato Hota"? "Yes, my Master, Tatanka Ska Son," answers Mato Hota as he, Luzahan and Ciqala, each look at one another nodding their heads in understanding.

Mato Hota continues speaking, "It is a good lesson You teach us with much wisdom, love and understanding of future things to come." Tatanka Ska Son says in His low deep Voice, "I leave you to finish your hunt. I will be by your side, even though you will not see Me. I will be with you always, as long as you believe in Me as Tatanka Ska Son, and My Father, Wakantanka, who watches all from Mahpiya, as the Great Spirit, the Creator and God." Tatanka Ska Son lifts off in slow flight, and silently vanishes into the rays of sunlight.

Until our next Campfire Story Telling – "The Hunt of the Bull Moose," may Wakantanka be with you.

Chapter 2

The Hunt of the Bull Moose

Ciqala (little one) speaks up in excitement to his two brothers, who stand transfixed looking in the direction of the new setting sun between the mountains into which Tatanka Ska Son (Son of Wakantanka, the Creator), Wanikiye (the Savior), has flown in ascension (flying upward, as if to the stars). He has come to this world in the form of a tatanka ska (white buffalo), to carry the stories of His Father, Wakantanka (God), who created Him in this form, to tell campfire stories to the Oglala (to scatter one's own) Lakota (the Siouan people) people, Oglala Lakota children and all who will listen. Ciqala speaks up, "My brother, Mato Hota (a grizzly bear) will Tatanka Ska Son come back"? Mato Hota, turns toward Ciqala and says in a reassuring tone of voice, "Tatanka Ska Son said, He would be by our side always and I believe in Him and so should we all, for we have flown with the eagles this day as no others. How could we doubt His Words? We must believe in Him and honor His Words."

Ciqala asks again, "I hear your words my brother, but do you think He will appear again soon"? Mato Hota answers, "I believe this Son of The Great Spirit, Tatanka Ska Son's Words. He will come back to teach us more, because He called us His brothers. Ciqala you must learn to trust your new Brother with deep love in your heart." Luzahan (swift) says, "I too believe our Big Brother, Tatanka Ska Son will return to be by our campfire and teach us His Father's Words."

Mato Hota changing the subject says, "We must start the hunt of the great moose before the mighty sun goes high above the mountains and he slips away into the tall trees from his feeding ground in the marsh downstream." The three young Oglala Lakota boys, gather wicat'es (an instrument with which to kill), their bows, wanjus (an arrow pouch; i.e. a quiver – English language) packed with hunting arrows, along with their spears, then they begin a slow trot downstream staying just inside the cover of tall trees near the swift water of the cold mountain stream. As they near the marsh area of the stream, it widens out into a large marsh area, with some tall grasses lining it.

This marsh has been created by some families of capas (beaver) who have made their lodges there.

The Hunt of the Bull Moose

The three young Oglala Lakota split off and quietly move toward the marsh from different directions. Their hope of finding the big moose feeding there appears likely, as they have seen him in this place before. They slowly approach the marsh and enter into the tall grass and slowly move forward. The three young hunters spot him feeding, just as they had hoped.

The big moose is ducking his head underwater to feed and then raises his massive head, takes in air through his nose as he chews a mouth full of water plants. He casually looks around and then puts his big head back underwater to feed again.

Mato Hota, motions by napeonwoglaka (sign language) directing Luzahan to go across the stream and come in from that direction, in case the moose sees them and tries to run away in his newly assigned position.

As Mato Hota and Ciqala crawl into a position about fifty feet away from the big moose, the moose raises his great head

crowned by huge antlers, up from underwater, they are dripping water from water-plants tangled in his huge rack of antlers, showing proudly from atop his head. He is a huge moose and he knows it. He is chewing water plants and looks around for a moment and then ducks his big head down underwater to gather more water-plants.

Mato Hota and Ciqala move in toward the shoreline and both raise their bows and pull back arrows at arms-length, taking aim at the big moose. All at once the big moose explodes up high in the water and wheels to run to the other shoreline. Mato Hota and Ciqala let loose their arrows. Ciqala barely misses with his hunting arrow, as he waited a moment longer than Mato Hota to react. Mato Hota's arrow flies straight and almost true, having missed hitting above the front leg and into the chest; it finds the neck of the big moose. Mato Hota's arrow in the big moose's thick muscled neck does not slow his flight as he bulls his way, pushing rapidly through the chest high water to the shore where Luzahan is waiting with his spear in hand.

Luzahan has been hiding behind a tree and waiting, as the big moose nears his hiding place at a full run. Just as the big moose is almost on Luzahan's hiding place he comes out from behind his tree of hiding and runs his spear with both hands deep into the chest of the big moose with all his might. Then he quickly dives out of the charging big bull moose's way, giving him a swift death, with little suffering, as Wakantanka would wish him to do.

The three young Oglala Lakota boys have their hands on the big moose lying before them and offer up thanks to Wakantanka for this wonderful gift, and then they start to whoop and holler and dance around in celebration of their first successful hunt of a big bull moose. Ciqala says, "We will be big talk in the village tonight." Luzahan says, "While they talk, I will eat, I am hungry now." Mato Hota says, "We must skin and quarter this kill and hang the meat we can't carry, high in the trees so the forest animals cannot eat our hunting gift from Wakantanka and His beloved Mother Earth. We will come back and gather the rest of this fine hunt later."

They begin the work of field dressing, by first hayuza (to take skin off anything) and then by cutting up the big moose into smaller sections to make transporting possible, because of the heavy weight of the huge animal. They load big pieces of the moose and carry about one third of the moose meat in its own tahalo (a hide) which they have hapašloka (to pull off the skin). They pack out all the meat they have strength enough to carry in the moose tahalo, slung in between two long poles crafted for carrying on their shoulders. The three Oglala Lakota boys gungagaya (proudly) march along, rotating the heavy load of moose meat between them, giving one a rest period, all the way back to their village singing songs of joy. It is a good day and a good time to live on Mother Earth.

The mighty sun is moving across the sky heading westward, to take a rest for the night letting all nature watch the stars dance and some will hunt, as is their custom, its work nearly done for this day, in this place, on Mother Earth as planned by Wakantanka.

The three young Oglala Lakota enter their village loaded down with moose meat riding in its own tahalo, which is strung from between two big poles carried over each shoulder, by Mato Hota at one end carrying a pole end on each shoulder. Luzahan and Ciqala are both at the other end of the two poles, each carrying a pole end over their shoulder. As they enter the village and pass by some women, the women begin a low chant, with smiles of approval for the three young hunters' first successful hunt of a big bull moose.

Soon many in the village gather to see the three young Oglala Lakota boys head toward the chief's tipi (teepee or tent or lodge) and stop before his large tipi. Now many villagers have gathered to see what the chief will say. The itancanka (the chief one, lord or master), Chief Matoskah (white bear) steps out of his lodge and greets the three young braves. Chief Matoskah says in a loud greeting for many to hear, "Welcome my son, Mato Hota, and brothers, let the women of the village prepare this fine fresh meat for all the village to share. Many moons have gone, since we have had moose by the campfires of our village. It is a good day."

Many women move in and take the moose meat from the young hunters, who now excuse themselves from their great Chief Matoskah, who is also, Mato Hota's father. The three head off to the nearby mountain stream to bathe off the sweat and dirt from the hunt, in its cool waters before the great sun sets behind the tall trees. They do not want to ohamna (smelling of skin - to smell badly) like the maka (the skunk or polecat) and offend the flavor smell coming from the cooked moose meat.

They want to share in this feast of moose meat given them by Wakantanka and this Mother Earth, without making others move away or hold their noses trying to eat this fine meal. To be clean is most important and the young maidens' notice everything and the three Oglala Lakota know they know. The cold water feels better, having this knowledge, but it is still very cold and they don't spend any time playing around, this is serious business.

Life has taken on new joy for the three young Oglala Lakota, who have had their first successful hunt, but the real joy is what

The Hunt of the Bull Moose

they have experienced with their new Brother Tatanka Ska Son, the Son of Wakantanka. How can they tell the villagers of their adventure high in the mountains flying with hundreds of eagles, who would believe such a tall tale, most especially coming from three young Oglala Lakota Indians trying to be known as braves among their tribe? The three would be silent for now and await the proper time for the telling of that story, which they alone share in secret as agreed.

There was great joy and visitation shared among the Oglala Lakota villagers, as they feasted on the hehak iktomi (a moose) meat, the three young Indians brought to the campfires of the Oglala Lakota on this clear star filled night. Embers from the campfires rose high in the air and some dancing was beginning among those who had finished eating.

Chief Matoskah slowly rose from his seated position and all went silent and still among the villagers as their great Chief Matoskah was about to speak. Chief Matoskah begins speaking, "It is a good day to be alive. Seeing my people living in peace in the land of our forefathers makes my heart sing with joy. Today is the day I call out with pride in my oldest and only son, Mato Hota, along with young Luzahan and Ciqala, who have brought the big moose to our village people. Now I say to all Oglala Lakota, Mato Hota, Luzahan, and Ciqala have come of age and are to be known among all of the people as brother Oglala Lakota braves. It is a good day and that is all I have to say." All in the village now begin yelling chants and awaci (to dance on anything or in honor of) in a celebration dance, honoring the three new braves.

Life among this band of Oglala Lakota Indians is sweet with the breath of spring bringing forth the goodness of plentiful game and harmony among the tribes. However, soon that would change, as men are prone to envy what others have, the cause for most wars, and this evil would soon visit the Oglala Lakota village with many raiding Anixshináabe named Chippewa. They are one of the most numerous indigenous people north of the Rio Grande and a great enemy of the Sioux Nation and its Oglala Lakota band.

Across the rocky mountains, an evil band of raiding Chippewa warriors, led by a ruthless warrior leader named Chief Bagwungijik (hole in the sky – Chippewa dialect) and unbeknown to any in the small Oglala Lakota village, they're are heading for Mato Hota's village on foot, pacing at a strong running trot as they move closer to his village. They can cover about twenty miles a day on foot and are fierce in appearance wearing colorful war paint, with feathers, bear claws and other bright ornaments, with the intent to steal the highly prized Oglala Lakota's trained riding horses.

The Oglala Lakota are the only Indian tribe who have horses in the region, which they took from early Spanish soldiers who attacked them long ago and lost their horses and their lives to the brave Oglala Lakota warriors of that day.

The evil raiding party is about five days away from the Oglala Lakota village, which is celebrating three Oglala Lakota youths to early manhood as Oglala Lakota braves with new stature and standing among the tribal members. They will be needed as the enemy tribe of the Chippewa's raiding party numbering sixty braves, draws nearer with each stride of their taha (deerskin) hanpa (moccasins) covered feet as they move in unison through the tall trees and large rock outcroppings at an easy steady trotting pace using short steps. As night falls, they stop and make campfires and eat before bedding down in their blankets laying on bunched up pine needles to keep them off the cold ground, providing good sleeping conditions, which they greatly needed after traveling all day on foot.

Days later, Chief Bagwungijik nears a main campfire and speaks to his Chippewa warriors, "We, my mighty warriors, are close to our enemy people of the Oglala Lakota. Before we takpe, (to come upon, attack) we will rest one more sunset near the Oglala Lakota and attack in the dawn of the first light, putting the sun into the eyes of our enemy. Kill many enemies and take all horses. Leave no horses for any who might live, to follow our trail." All the raiding Chippewa braves, cheer the evil leader Chief Bagwungijik's spoken words, that of a great warrior, as if they came from 'a hole in the sky'. Evil is heading for the happy village of the Oglala Lakota, who are now soundly sleeping in their blankets.

The usual guards are stationed (posted) outside the Oglala Lakota village, listening for any movement of man or beast, hearing only the sounds of nature at peace; they only hear some insects singing a night song. Soon the three new Oglala Lakota braves will share in this trusted duty to protect the village, by taking turns standing guard, which is considered a high honor to be chosen to serve on guard duty. Watching out for the safety of the entire village is a duty of honor and carries a heavy weight of responsibility. Only the best and trusted braves serve as night guards. In the hills, other eyes are watching from afar at this time with keen interest...

Until our next Campfire Story Telling – "Mato Hota Takes a Prisoner," which tells about Wakantanka and His Son, Tatanka Ska Son, Wanikiye (Savior). May Wakantanka Bless You and always remember He loves you, because you are very special to Him.

Three Lakota warriors returning to their village

Chapter 3

Mato Hota Takes a Prisoner

It is early in the morning sunlight that the Chippewa (Anishináabe meaning 'original person') warriors are nearing the Oglala (to scatter one's own) Lakota (the Siouan people) village and take-up hiding places among the tall pine trees, about a mile away. They are making ready their weapons and have spread out in a large front line as they settle down to rest and await the signal by Chief Bagwungijik (hole in the sky – Chippewa dialect) to advance in the attack on the unsuspecting small Oglala Lakota village.

Mato Hota (the grizzly bear), Luzahan (swift) and Ciqala

(little one), head out to go fishing in a large mountain lake nearby from their village to the east. They are playing a game of "Stalking" they have made up. It is a practice of hunting in silence. It is almost like our game of Hide and Seek, but the difference being the first one to make noise, is stalked by the others and jumped on, as if by an enemy. It is a good practice, a game in the life skills an Indian brave must learn to survive in the wilds of nature's bread basket, provided by Mother Earth.

Being a good hunter is highly respected by other tribe members, and these three new braves will work hard and practice whenever they can to be held in high standing among their Oglala Lakota tribal members. To hold honor among the Oglala Lakota people is of true value one can hold, when it is gone you have lost all the respect of the tribe and given a new name of disrespect to carry until you redeem yourself.

Mato Hota is thinking to himself as he slips through the brush very quietly, that since he helped bring in the great moose, some of the young maidens in the tribe have been staring cantognagya (in a loving manner) and he is amused by this new attention directed toward him, and he finds it strangely pleasing. Mato Hota is moving very slowly forward at a low crawl past a tree and he sees a foot with a taha (deerskin) hanpa (moccasins) sticking out from behind a large pine tree about twenty feet out in front of him. Mato Hota comes to a pataka (to come to a stand, as a horse does) instantly. He does not recognize the taha hanpa as one Luzahan or Ciqala are wearing. He slowly moves his spear he uses for fishing and small game closer to his body. His heart is racing now as he does not know if this is an enemy or friend, but he feels whoever it is; they are spying on his tribe or hunting like him. Mato Hota has to control his breathing in his excitement and starts to think of what to do.

Mato Hota Takes a Prisoner

He decides to rush the unknown Indian brave, surprise him by placing his fishing spear in his back and take him prisoner and possibly learn who he is and what he is doing so near his Oglala Lakota village. Mato Hota stands up and silently creeps up on the prone figure of a big young brave. Suddenly he rushes in on the unknown brave and places his fishing spear against the brave's back. The brave freezes, knowing he better not move or he could feel more from the fishing spear head with three points pinning him to the ground. Mato Hota moves his spear with sharp fishing points to the back of the neck of the unknown brave and has him turn over to face him, by using his foot to turn him over.

Mato Hota speaks quietly, but with strength in his voice, "Stay still and live. Who are you"? The young brave does not speak out or answer. Mato Hota studies the looks and dress of the young brave and recognizes this brave must be a Chippewa, part of an enemy tribe of his people. After gathering up the captive's weapons, he uses napeonwoglaka (to use sign language), indicating for the Chippewa brave to stand up and to move out in the direction of the Oglala Lakota village.

Luzahan and Ciqala hear the noises of the two braves passing by their hidden positions and quietly join their new brave brother Mato Hota, who has now captured his first enemy and surely earned his new title, as an Oglala Lakota brave. They also, point their spears toward the Chippewa warrior and have surrounded him, keeping a close watch on his every move, as the three young braves move him quietly toward their Oglala Lakota village.

Mato Hota marches the Chippewa warrior straight to his father, Chief Matoskah (white bear), who is sitting in front of his tipi (teepee or tent or lodge). Other Oglala Lakota braves have gathered around the captive Chippewa warrior, some are yelling and whopping loudly, putting fear into Mato Hota's prisoner. They grab him and tie him standing with his back to a pole in the ground. Chief Matoskah uses napeonwoglaka language attempting to ask the Chippewa warrior his name. He remains silent.

Some braves bring wood and place it around him and then one Oglala Lakota brave standing nearby, hands a petuspe (a firebrand with which to start another fire) to Chief Matoskah. The chief signs with his hands again and waves the petuspe back and forth in front of the Chippewa brave's face asking for his name as he slowly kneels to light the wood around the Chippewa enemy's feet. The Chippewa brave, realizing he is about to die a terrible death, quickly answers his name, "Animikii" (thunder – Chippewa dialect).

Chief Matoskah straightens up and looks at the Chippewa brave very closely. He is wearing war paint and has eagle feathers running across the front of his long black hair and is dressed in a taha (deerskin) shirt and pants and he also wears many beaded necklaces around his neck, some with bear claws and small quail feathers. He appears to Chief Matoskah as a brave in standing among his band of Chippewa and he must be of some importance or standing among his tribe. The chief orders three braves to take Animikii to a tipi, tie him up, and guard him closely. He also instructs two young maidens to prepare food and water for the Chippewa prisoner and to treat him with yuonihanyan (honoring, treat politely). His orders are carried out, as three braves take the Chippewa warrior away to a lodge nearby, with two maidens following behind them.

Chief Matoskah calls all the braves in the village to his campfire. Chief Matoskah speaks, "My son, Mato Hota, has taken a Chippewa warrior prisoner. Mato Hota has told me that

Mato Ḣota Takes a Prisoner

this Chippewa was lying in the tall trees scouting our village. He is a Chippewa enemy scout. I know not how many warriors are coming against us. Canška (red-legged hawk), you and Wanbligleška (the spotted eagle), go scout where the sun comes over the mountain and find our enemies strength and return swiftly on our fastest šunkawakans (horses) and take iwaglamnas (an extra or fresh horse) and travel with the wind in your face, that the Chippewa will not smell your šunkawakans.

"All other braves move the šunkawakans, children and women to our hiding place in the great cave, ten braves to stand guard over the cave entrance. All other braves to stand behind the trees and boulders near the stream and to takpe (to come upon, attack) as the Chippewa cross over our stream. We take them as they cross slowly in the swift waters. It will be a good fighting place for us to meet the enemy."

All the braves of the Oglala Lakota village, run to find their weapons and then take defending positions near the village, behind trees and large boulders lining the swift stream's shoreline and all stay on high alert for the expected enemy Chippewa's coming takpe. There is no time for a war dance, and all Oglala Lakota warriors must stand ready for fighting. The village is buzzing with action, like a large bee hive with a waowešica (a bear, in general) tearing it apart looking for a sweet snack of honey to put on some extra fat for winter.

Mato Ḣota asked his father, Chief Matoskah, "Why did you not kill our enemy Chippewa scout, called Animikii, he who spied on our people"? Chief Matoskah answers his son, "To me, there is no honor in killing one who cannot fight back. I say also, he may serve us later." "Good words my wise father, only in honor wowitanwaya (to glory in) can a wawašagya (to render worthless) brave be worthy of being known as a brave in good standing," replies Mato Hota. "You are learning brave son, now go find knowledge from your captive," orders Chief Matoskah.

Meanwhile, Chief Bagwungijik and his band of Chippewa raiders are on the move toward the Oglala Lakota village one half day's distance on foot. Chief Bagwungijik has sent two braves to look for his missing son, Animikii, who has not returned to him. The two Chippewa braves returned with word that they have seen signs of foot prints in the pine needles, which shows he has been taken by Oglala Lakota scouts. Chief Bagwungijik becomes šakehute s'e hingle (angry as a bear), as he leads his raiding band swiftly through the deep forest of tall pines, thinking of his son, Animikii, and what may have happened to him, and he wants a blood revenge, a watogya (to spoil, ruin; to take vengeance, retaliate, to kill) a powerful response to his son's capture and possible torture by his enemy the Oglala Lakota people.

Canška and Wanbligleška are seated on their horses watching the movement of their enemy, from a tall tree covered hill. They have spotted the advancing Chippewa raiders and estimate their numbers and rate of advance to their village. They turn and walk their horses slowly and quietly over the hill and then ride at gallop —the fastest gait or speed a horse can run— to report their scouting results to Chief Matoskah, not sparing any of their horses in their return to their Oglala Lakota village.

The two scouts ride into the Oglala Lakota village, with their šunkawakans panting from the hard ride the braves have given them, with their iwaglamnas (an extra or spare horse) horses and their personal horses trailing behind them. They dismount, turning their tired horses over to other braves to be cooled down —by walking them for a while— then they are to be watered, bathed and fed. The two scouts enter the chief's tipi in a rush,

Mato Hota Takes a Prisoner

after calling out his name to announce themselves.

Canška speaks up quickly, "My chief, Chippewa enemy raiders by our count are about sixty strong and are closing within a half day, all running a steady even trotting pace, all on foot. They may rest before they attack us, that is all I have to say, great Chief Matoskah." "This is a good sign for fighting; the village is ready for zuya (to make war). The enemy count of Chippewa may have more braves, but none can fight as we do on horses and on foot. Rest and then join your brothers and make ready to fight the evil coming against us," says Chief Matoskah in a commanding tone of voice.

The Oglala Lakota villagers are prepared for battle. Some as ordered by Chief Matoskah are standing by their horses on the west side of the villages numerous tipis, ready to attack the enemy on horseback if any get through the braves on the battle line near the mountain stream. Others on foot are lined up behind trees and boulders near the shore of the cold swift moving waters of the mountain stream. It is a long night for the Oglala Lakota braves, as they wait for the Chippewa to takpe (to come upon, attack).

Chief Matoskah has requested that the raiding warrior leader be captured, if possible, for he believes the Chippewa brave, Animikii, which Mato Hota has captured, could be Chief Bagwungijik's son. That is what Mato Hota believes, after using napeonwoglaka to communicate with Animikii (thunder – Chippewa dialect); wakinyan (thunder – Lakota dialect). Mato Hota treated the Chippewa captive Animikii with kindness and respect and was able to find out that he was in good standing with the leader, Chief Bagwungijik, and plainly not, an ordinary scout among his tribe. This was good to learn, Chief Matoskah told Mato Hota this raid could be happening earlier in the day and he was right.

Chief Bagwungijik calls the raiding band of Chippewa together and he instructs them in his plan of attack. His warriors are to quietly approach the village spread out in a long line and when given his signal, all are to rush in on the enemy at the same time to overwhelm the enemy with what Chief Bagwungijik thinks is their superior numbers in a surprise takpe. That is the evil battle plan Chief Bagwungijik has in his mind and has given this pre-planned battle formation instruction to his braves.

All Chippewa braves, less a few guards, are hidden among the trees about one quarter of a mile from the eastern edge of the mountain stream as the sun sets in the western sky. They are gathering back their strength, with much needed sleep before they takpe.

All are asleep, however not Chief Bagwungijik who is worried about his son and what his son, Animikii, may be suffering at the hands of the Oglala Lakota. His night is long and sleepless, for he is filled with anguish and rage and all sleep escapes him.

Morning light is breaking through the eastern sky and the raiding band of Chippewa are on the move toward the Oglala Lakota village lead by Chief Bagwungijik, who is moving at a steady pace, in spite of a sleepless night. He is fully fueled by hate for his enemy, as he moves forward. When the raiders reach about seventy-five feet from the eastern edge of the swift mountain stream they must cross, Chief Bagwungijik signals his warriors to line up side by side about five feet apart, as he had previously planned and instructed them. He signals the raiders to attack. The Chippewa braves are at a full run closing the distance from the western shore of the fast-moving water separating them

Mato Hota Takes a Prisoner

from their goal, horses, maiden slaves and revenge.

Chief Matoskah and his braves are aware of the attacking Chippewa as they approach the village; his scouts have been silently watching them and reporting to Chief Matoskah all night long. This was done by sneaking by the forward night guards as the rest of the Chippewa warriors slept in their blankets. Chief Matoskah has given the command to hold from killing until they have his signal to takpe.

The first line of Oglala Lakota defenders will wait until given the signal from Chief Matoskah to first engage the enemy with arrows and spears, after they have reached the middle of the fast water of the mountain stream. Then they are to retreat to the other side of the village, as the braves on horseback charge into the fight, loosing arrows, spears upon the toka (one of a foreign or hostile nation, an enemy). Then the braves on foot are to come in behind the charging braves on horseback and finish the battle with their wicat'e (an instrument with which to kill).

It is a great battle plan, for Chief Matoskah is a great chief and has fought many times before in battle. All the villagers are afraid, but trust their leader, Chief Matoskah and his war plan, for he has never been defeated in battle.

Chief Bagwungijik gives the signal to launch the attack, running fast and then slowing as he reaches the fast-moving waters of the cold mountain stream. He and all the others are almost to the middle of the stream, wading as fast as they can in the cold fast waters of the mountain stream. The Oglala Lakota braves on foot prepare to shoot their arrows, some planning their best distance, to throw their spears as the enemy closes in. Just before the Chippewa reach the middle of the stream, a bright blue ray of light hits the western side of the stream and startles the Chippewa warriors, who stop their forward movement in the knee-deep water.

Then, the stream suddenly turns to ice, freezing all the Chippewa warriors in its cold icy grip. They all are yelling and screaming now, as the cold bites them, being frozen in place by some unknown power and realizing they are sitting ducks for Oglala Lakota spears and arrows. How can this be happening thinks Chief Bagwungijik?

Tatanka Ska Son appears in the blue beam of light and all within sight of Him are astounded and frozen in place with fear, afraid of this unknown power appearing before them. No Oglala Lakota spears or arrows are launched at the enemy, all is still, all is silent. In His deep Voice heard by all in their own language, Tatanka Ska Son speaks up, "I say to all Chippewa raiders, beware of your evil intent and ways of war against My people, the Oglala Lakota. Come forward to Me, Bagwungijik."

Instantly, Chief Bagwungijik is freed from the ice which had locked him in place along with all his warriors. Chief Bagwungijik begins crossing to Tatanka Ska Son. "Drop your weapons Bagwungijik and come in before Me, only in peace." Chief Bagwungijik drops his spear, wicat'e and then knife in the mountain stream as he moves toward Tatanka Ska Son. "Matoskah, you also, come to face Me with empty hands," orders Tatanka Ska Son.

Both understand Tatanka Ska Son as He speaks to them, even though they speak different language. They understand Tatanka Ska Son, for Tatanka Ska Son knows all languages and has all

Mato Hota Takes a Prisoner

knowledge, for He is the Son of Wakantanka. The two chiefs stand before Tatanka Ska Son in fear and amazement at the presence of the giant white buffalo with big blue eyes, who speaks to them and has appeared before them in a most astounding way.

"I say to you and all hear Me now, I am the Son of 'Wakantanka, God, the Creator', you will call Me, Tatanka Ska Son from this day forward. I have come from Mahpiya (Heaven), where My Father, Wakantanka, God, the Creator lives, to tell the story of My Father's will. Bagwungijik, you have come to harm in an act of vengeance, and steal horses and take maiden slaves from My Chosen People the Oglala, the Oglala of the Lakota Nation. This will not stand. Matoskah, will give you one of your greatest gifts in this life, he will give this gift freely. Mato Hota, —speaking in only Lakota dialect— bring Animikii and stand him unbound by his father," commands Tatanka Ska Son. Mato Hota runs to the tipi holding his Chippewa prisoner, enters, unties Animikii —who has heard the deep Voice of Tatanka Ska Son, but does not understand His Words spoken to Mato Hota— unlike all the Oglala Lakota villagers, who do understand His Words.

Mato Hota brings Animikii forward, places him by Chief Bagwungijik's side and returns to stand by his father's side. Neither Chippewa, reunited father or son make a move, as they are frozen in fear standing before Tatanka Ska Son.

"I speak to you now Bagwungijik, the great chief among the Oglala Lakota, Matoskah has spared your son, Animikii, as I have spared you and your Chippewa warriors by Matoskah's example of woonšila (mercy) and My love of those My Father Wakantanka has chosen to be My people. Let it be known by all, the people of the Oglala Lakota Nation are My people, the chosen people of Wakantanka. I will ask Matoskah to bring two of his finest šungbloka (the male horse or dog) and two šungwinyela (a mare horse – female horse) in foal —carrying a baby horse in their belly, soon becoming mothers in the spring. Matoskah, I ask you to give them to Bagwungijik as a gift to the Chippewa tribe. If Matoskah will do this, I will be pleased by his towaonšila (his mercy) and he will be rewarded by My Father Wakantanka." Speaking once again, in His low deep Voice, "I, Tatanka Ska Son have spoken, honor Me, and honor My Words."

Chief Matoskah drops to his knees and the entire Oglala Lakota band kneel, as well. Chief Matoskah asks Tatanka Ska Son, "May I speak, Oh Great Tatanka Ska Son"? Tatanka Ska Son replies, "You may speak My brother." "Mato Ḣota, Luzahan, Ciqala, Canška and Wanbligleška, bring the horses Tatanka Ska Son has ask of me to give them as a gift to Chief Bagwungijik," orders Chief Matoskah. Four Chippewa braves frozen in ice with all the other braves are freed from its cold icy grip. Tatanka Ska Son commands, "Come forward Chippewa braves now freed —from the ice bound stream— come empty handed and stand by your chief, Bagwungijik."

The four Chippewa braves now free of the ice, approach after dropping their weapons into the mountain stream, with a look of amazement written in their faces and they cross the stream and stand by their leader still frozen, but now only frozen in fear. The five young Oglala Lakota braves lead the horses by their bridles and reins, made of ptehašla (buffalo hide from which the hair has been removed) and give them as a gift of friendship to Chief Bagwungijik and his son, Animikii. These four Chippewa braves will lead them back to their village in peace.

No words are spoken by Chief Bagwungijik or the other Chippewa standing in fear of this Great White Buffalo, who

Mato Hota Takes a Prisoner

speaks all languages and performs magical feats and appears to command all. Tatanka Ska Son speaks, "Bagwungijik, you will take the gift of your son Animikii's life, given back to you by Matoskah and Mato Hota, his son, he who captured your son, Animikii, and also, spared his life. Take also, these fine horses, a gift from Matoskah. Treat these fine horses well and they will serve you and the Chippewa people well, soon all will ride and never be on foot again, unless that is their choice. They will multiply and serve the Chippewa nation, who now walk Mother Earth on foot.

"Go now in peace, never to war against My People the Oglala of the Lakota Nation after this day. This is a great day of blessing, because of Matoskah's wisdom in sparing the life of your son, Animikii, and all other Chippewa braves standing by you this day. Go in peace and do not return, except in friendship and love as a brother to My Chosen People. Keep My Words Wakan (Holy) as I have spoken." Tatanka Ska Son slowly lifts off and flies away into the sunlight.

All the remaining Chippewa warriors are instantly freed from the ice that bound them and they watch as the remaining ice flows downstream. Chief Bagwungijik and Animikii now hug one another and each one nod in a gesture of thanks to Chief Matoskah and Mato Hota. Then they turn and lead the new gift of horses to join the other Chippewa warriors in the mountain stream, who raise their hands in a sign of respect and all slowly disappear into the forest. What a story they will have to tell by their campfires upon returning to their Chippewa village.

Tatanka Ska Son speaks only to the ears of Chief Matoskah from afar, "Matoskah, I am pleased with you this day. Your son, Mato Ḣota, brothers Luzahan and Ciqala, have stories to tell you, you will honor Me by passing the stories of this day and the stories they tell you, down to the campfires of all that come after you. I, Tatanka Ska Son have spoken."

Chief Matoskah answers silently from his mind 'Your Words will be done, just as they have been spoken'. All the Oglala Lakota villagers, in unison, give up a great sound of awe, only walled off by the sweet sounds of the fast waters and their ever-singing sounds of peace. Chief Matoskah says, "Mato Ḣota, Luzahan, and Ciqala come to my tipi, we have much to speak of this day."

And speak they will, for there is much to say in future campfire stories. Until our next Campfire Story Telling – "A Great Bear Chase," may Wakantanka Bless You always, for you are surely loved by Him.

Young Oglala Lakota Girl

The Chosen Ones Oglala Warriors

Whitetail Deer

Chapter 4

A Great Bear Chase

The Itancanka (the chief one, lord or master), Chief Matoskah (white bear), his son Mato Hota (a grizzly bear), along with Luzahan (swift) and Ciqala (little one), are seated around the great chief's campfire in his tipi (teepee or tent or lodge). The three new braves have each told their story of their encounter and meeting with Tatanka Ska Son (the Savior) while on their hunt for the great moose and how Tatanka Ska Son, Son of Wakantanka (The Great Spirit, the Creator, God), who is appearing in the form of a tatanka ska (white buffalo) saved them from the mighty golden colored mato hota. Also, how He took them to fly with the mighty eagles in the high mountains surrounded by white clouds.

Chief Matoskah was awed by the story telling and understood why the three had not told their stories before, even he could hardly believe that which Tatanka Ska Son had done for his Oglala (to scatter one's own) tribe and the Lakota (the Siouan people) people. He saved many lives of the Oglala Lakota and most likely, many of the Chippewa (Anishináabe meaning 'original person'), the warriors from across the mountains, were also saved, as told in our previous Campfire Story, "Mato Hota Takes a Prisoner."

The Chippewa would not come here to war on the Oglala Lakota ever again, for they have seen the power of Tatanka Ska Son and would heed His Words and tell this great story to their people by their many campfires for many moons to come. Tatanka Ska Son was to become known by other tribes and would visit them someday to spread the Words of His Father's Will, but that is another campfire story, yet to be told.

As the sun was setting over the western sky, all the Oglala Lakota villagers were gathered by a large campfire and Chief Matoskah called on Mato Hota, Luzahan and Ciqala to tell their stories one by one, as each had experienced. Later in the night, when the three new braves finished telling their campfire stories, all the tribe members were silent, showing respect for them, as they would from this day forward. All because, the braves were a friend and brother of Tatanka Ska Son, who the villagers at this time, believe is truly the Son of The Great Spirit coming from Mahpiya (Heaven).

He who has come to earth, as a wakan (sacred one) in the form of a tatanka ska comes to teach the Oglala and the Lakota

Nation. All the villagers then began to perform the Wiwanyank Wacipi (the Sundance), and chant praises to Chief Matoskah for saving the village and to the three Oglala Lakota braves, now brothers to Tatanka Ska Son, Mato Ḣota, Luzahan and Ciqala each of their very own village. Great joy filled the hearts of the Oglala Lakota people as they danced the wacipi and chanted deep into the cool night air. All the Oglala Lakota villagers are sharing the feeling of warmth in their hearts on this most special of nights.

The next morning finds Mato Ḣota, Luzahan and Ciqala, shooting down the swift waters of the big stream that flows by their village in Mato Ḣota's borrowed birch bark canoe. The outside covering of the birch tree is used in making canoes, — which is flexible and water proof. Mato Ḣota is in the rear of the canoe paddling and steering with his paddle, with Ciqala in the middle and Luzahan up in the nose of the canoe, watching for rocks and other obstacles, as they race through the rapids. All three young braves, paying close attention to the rapids they are shooting through, paddling very hard to keep control of their canoe.

What the young braves do not see is a very hungry huge brown mato ḣota who has spotted them a short distance back up stream above the rapids and is racing along the edge between rocks and trees, looking for a way to catch the three, before they are out of his reach.

Luzahan is looking for boulders and rocks in the narrowing of the mountain stream, forcing the water to kaluza (to flow rapidly, as water) as part of the rapids, these are the worst they have encountered so far. It is exciting and a challenge to the new braves, to run this part of what is now a dangerous part of the cold mountain stream. They still do not know what danger is following them at a full run and it is not, a soft little rabbit intending a soft nuzzle, which is stalking them.

The stream meets another swift running stream around a sharp curve between two cliff faces and both together become a raging river. Just before the two streams merge is a sharp bend, which Luzahan cannot see around.

The cliffs on each side end and a big log has fallen across the narrow rushing stream ahead of the three braves. As they paddle around the bend in the rapids, Luzahan sees the log and a huge brown mato hota perched on the log, waiting for them when he yells, "Awašicahowaya (to cry out on account of), wakita (to look out for, to watch) the hinsko (so big, so large) mato hota." There is no time to avoid the great mato hota, who swings his big right paw down and takes a swipe at Luzahan, which nearly catches him, but he ducks quickly to his right. The mato hota misses Luzahan and catches the port (left side) side of the canoe with his long claws, turning it over, dumping the young braves in the rapids just out of reach of the huge mato hota.

The huge mato hota turns and watches from his log perch, as the young braves disappear down river, struggling against the rapids as they bob up and down, just missing some boulders jutting above the rapids in their wild ride, being carried swiftly in the white water of the rapids down river fighting for their lives.

Ciqala is in front of Mato Hota, as they are being swept down river and he seems yugo (to be fatigued) and finally goes under water. Mato Hota swims to where Ciqala disappeared and dives under the rapid fast flowing water. Luzahan does not see this happen and when he turns to look for them, his brothers are nowhere to be seen.

Luzahan is very scared and worried for the safety of his brothers, and heads for the shore to his right, hoping he can make it before the cold water takes his life, then he will search up river to look for Mato Hota and Ciqala, whom he hopes went ashore before him and for that he is becoming less hopeful, as he swims fighting the rapids toward the shore. He finally reaches shore, thinking bad thoughts which were creeping into his mind about his Oglala Lakota brothers, when he hears Mato Hota, yelling downstream from him. He is helping Ciqala to shore and safety.

The three young braves having reached shore are cold and exhausted, so they climb in between large boulders and lay down to catch the fresh mountain air by taking big breaths. They are thankful to Wakantanka to be free from the cold-water rapids.

Mato Hota says, "I have lost my father's canoe and now we must return without fish or his canoe, he will not be pleased. I feel good, that we all live to tell our story of the great rapids running fast over the rocks." Luzahan makes iyaš'a-pi (an acclamation) and he continues, "Don't forget the big brown mato hota trying to eat me for his shrunken belly, to be big again." With that said, the three manage a weak laugh.

The laughter is short lived, as Ciqala spots something coming down the river. The three are hoping that somehow, Chief Matoskah's overturned canoe may have been hung-up on rocks and just broke free and was floating to them, but soon they realize it is moving toward them with determination. It is the dreaded killer mato hota swimming fast, his eyes locked on them. Luzahan yells, "Run for your lives my brothers."

The three are making good time among the tall pine trees heading toward their village, when they hear the mato hota closing in behind them, and he is gaining on them fast, for he is strong and mighty.

The three braves have lost their weapons in the river rapids and have no way to fight this brown mato hota. In a last attempt at defense against the great mato hota, the young braves stop and pick up rocks to face this great mato hota together, in a last stand against this huge ferocious killer of all that lives in the deep woods.

Suddenly, as the big attacking mato hota is almost upon them, a lightning strike hits the ground between the young braves and charging great brown mato hota, making a deep hole in the ground and knocking the young braves off their feet. The great mato hota cannot stop his charge and falls into the deep pit caused by the lightning strike.

Mato Hota, Luzahan and Ciqala get up and check themselves for any signs of injury and each other and to see if they have any burns from the lightning strike. They are unhurt and slowly creep up on the edge of the deep hole in the ground and peer in. The great brown mato hota has been stunned by his fall into the deep hole, he regains his footing, then shakes the loose dirt off his long brown fur, some of which has been singed and he stands up on his hind legs and tries to climb out.

The young braves quickly back up from the edge of the hole. Luzahan says to Mato Hota, "We can stone (kill with rocks) the great mato hota with big rocks, before he can hurt any braves out hunting in his hunting grounds." Mato Hota says, "Let us watch him and see if he is able to get out and try to attack us again. If he looks like he can't get out, maybe we should leave him alone to his tokata (in the future, or the future).

"If we start hitting him with rocks, he may find the strength in this torturous pain and suffering and it could build up his anger to come up after us with new strength in his great body." "Wise words spoken Mato Hota, you saved me from the cold waters and I don't want to be a warm meal for mighty mato hota in the hole," adds Ciqala in his short speech, showing gratefulness to Mato Hota.

All of the big mato hota's frantic efforts give way to exhaustion, as he claws at the loose dirt on the walls of the deep pit, he is a prisoner of and he ceases his frantic efforts to climb out. Luzahan says, "Let's leave him in the makok'e (a dug-out, a pit) so we can pae (to inflict punishment) on this evil one, and he will die without water."

Mato Hota has noticed that the big brown mato hota has only been reaching up to try and crawl out using mostly, his right paw. Mato Hota says, "Look, the great mato hota is hurt, I have seen, he cannot use his big left paw. He must have hurt himself when he fell in the makok'e made by the great lightning strike. Even though he is a mean creature, hunger is the itancanka (the chief one, lord and master) of his evil ways. I don't like to see any of the Creator's animals suffer, with no chance to survive and heal or being given a chance for Mother Earth to make them whole again."

"I have a way," exclaims Ciqala, "let's drop a log with limbs down for the mato hota to climb out and then run fast to our village. Evil one is hurt and will not follow my brothers." The three braves nod to each other in agreement. Mato Hota says, "Ciqala, you are speaking wisdom more each day, you make me

The Chosen Ones Oglala Warriors

feel gunga (proud) to call you, brother." Ciqala smiles a broad face smile that last longer than usual. It is a good blessing to receive praise from those whom you respect; it makes the heart grow wahtinyan (to be fond of).

The three look around, through the tall trees for a fallen log that has not become rotten with age lying on the ground. They find a tree that has been hit by lightning at its base, which has split, but is slowly dying, its leaves of yellow showing its slow death. The three see that it is close to falling over, so they work hard to push it over having no other way to take the tree down, as they cannot chop it down without a sharp stone edged tomahawk, which are now lost forever in the rapids.

The braves struggle to get the tree down and when they knock it over it breaks in half. This is good oglu (luck, fortune) and it makes it easier to drag it in place by the edge of the hole. The great mato hota eyes the young braves as they look in at him sitting on its big haunches moaning in pain and looking acantešilyakel (sadly or sorrowfully for) his bad situation sitting in the bottom of the deep hole. The three watch him for some time, as he moans and sits very still. Mato Hota says, "Let's push the broken tree down now and run fast, before he recovers his power and climbs out to eat us."

They push the tree down on an angle to the bottom of the pit. Surprise! Before they can start to run, the huge wise mato hota is up the slanted tree in a flash, using his great strength he has regained, and is quickly upon them. Instantly, a blue flash in the shape of a blue light tube, appears between the huge mato hota and Ciqala, who is nearest to the big gapping mouth of

A Great Bear Chase

the mato hota, which is gaped wide open, dripping saliva, and is about to bite him. Tatanka Ska Son appears in the blue light between Ciqala and the attacking brown mato hota.

The huge mato hota stops in his tracks and Tatanka Ska Son says in His deep Voice, "Do not run, stand and behold." The huge mato hota has also understood Tatanka Ska Son and stands still, as do Mato Hota, Luzahan and Ciqala. Tatanka Ska Son moves in on the huge brown mato hota and gently nuzzles his chest —while he is standing upright on his hind legs— with His big horned head of white fur and black fur covered ears. The huge mato hota calmly sits down in front of Tatanka Ska Son and remains totally still.

Tatanka Ska Son turns and walks to each young brave and nuzzles them softly with his huge white head and they kneel down in reverence to Him. Tatanka Ska Son speaks to the young braves, "My Father, Wakantanka (the Creator, God), and I have seen your onšila (to have mercy on) and kindness toward your enemy in the face of great danger and we are greatly pleased. Get up and go hug the huge brown mato hota in a show of friendship, for he is now forever your friend and you need not fear him."

The three stand up and Mato Hota is first to walk over to the huge brown mato hota, who has closed his big mouth by this time, and hugs him by his great tahuhute (nape of the neck) neck. To Mato Hota's great surprise the brown mato hota gives him a big friendly soft "waowešica (a bear, in general) hug." The huge mato hota softly moans through his big nose, as each brave gives him a hug around his massive furry neck. Luzahan and Ciqala, also, both get a big "bear hug" from the huge brown mato hota.

Tatanka Ska Son speaks, "From this day, call brown mato hota by his new name Mato Hota (a grizzly bear) Titakuye (immediate relatives) your new brother. Rise up Mato Ḣota Titakuye, you are healed and saved by the three new brothers of the forest and you must never igni (to stalk game) or hunt, any who walk wohlepe s'e (standing upright) on two legs as human beings do, they are My Chosen People of the Oglala Lakota Nation.

"Mato Ḣota Titakuye, you will go and hunt the animals of the forest and plants of the land, which I have chosen for you to hunt and live on, now go in peace. Mato Ḣota Titakuye, your shoulder has been made okiyuta (to heal up) from your fall into the pit and your scorched fur has been restored for many winter's warmth, which was caused by lightning My Father sent to stop your evil ways against His People, know this and remember My Words."

Mato Ḣota Titakuye, stands upon his four big legs, nods in an understanding way and growls in a low friendly tone, bows down on his front paws to honor Tatanka Ska Son. He then turns and lumbers off into the deep forest of tall trees.

Tatanka Ska Son speaks to the three young Oglala Lakota braves and directly to Mato Ḣota, "I have restored your father's canoe and weapons to the riverside near here, go and claim them and return to your village and tell this story, just as it happened to you, to all other villagers who are beginning to believe in My Father, the Creator, and His Son, Tatanka Ska Son, for We are real, as you can see with your own eyes."

The three braves move swiftly to recover their canoe and weapons and can hardly contain their great joy, and to be able to tell this story of honor, kindness and onšila, —truly the real values of wealth of one's life— which can be measured in any

A Great Bear Chase

person or animal of the Creator on this His life giving Mother Earth.

The three braves hurry back to their village portaging — carrying a canoe or boat— their chief's canoe. They are carrying much more than a canoe, now being armed with more campfire stories to tell about Tatanka Ska Son and the great brown mato hota, now to be known as Mato Hota Titakuye (a grizzly bear relative), their new friend and now grizzly bear brother.

You will hear more in the following campfire stories. Before you sleep remember, all the good things in life were given to you by Wakantanka and His Son, Tatanka Ska Son (Jesus), thank Him in your prayers and for Mahpiya's sake, be good.

Until the next Campfire Story Telling — "Fishing, Bears and Wolves," may Wakantanka's Blessings be upon you and all your oyate (tribe).

Tatanka

Oglala Lakota trailing out on a tatanka hunt

Chapter 5

Fishing, Bears and Wolves

Three young braves slowly walk into their Oglala (to scatter one's own) Lakota (the Siouan people) village looking very tired, but happy to be home safe, and each one carried a great story to share with Chief Matoskah (white bear). They headed straight for the chief's tipi (teepee or tent or lodge), where Chief Matoskah welcomed them in by his warm fire. Each young brave related their story of the great brown mato hota (a grizzly bear) and his personal encounter with this fearsome creature and being saved by Tatanka Ska Son (Son of Wakantanka The Great Spirit), in the form of a tatanka ska (white buffalo).

Mato Hota (named after a grizzly bear) son of Chief Matoskah, was first to story his tell. "My father, you should have seen how the great mato hota was made to become our titakuye (immediate relatives). He will never attack us or any tribe member, if they see him in the hunting grounds of our forefathers, and he will be their friendly mato hota titakuye (grizzly bear – the immediate relatives) or grizzly brother. We must tell our story, so no one will attack our new mato hota titakuye (grizzly brother) when hunting."

Chief Matoskah says, "It shall be done this night. I, Chief Matoskah, will call for a campfire council among all the braves, let that be known, that is all I have to say." The three young braves, after all have given their stories to Chief Matoskah, go out and spread the news of a campfire council to be held end of day and all braves must come, women and all other children are welcome and encouraged to hear the stories of the three braves and the words of their Chief Matoskah. All braves must attend as Chief Matoskah has spoken and it will be so.

As night closes in upon the happy village of the Oglala Lakota, the villagers are entranced by the great stories, the three young braves have told them by the giant campfire in the middle of the village. Mato Hota, Luzahan (swift) and Ciqala (little one) don't realize at this time, but the people of the village are beginning to show iwanglaka (to have regard for one's own) toward the three young braves. They are considered truly chosen by Tatanka Ska Son as brothers and close companions and the stories the three young braves have told are held in great regard iwanglaka by many in the Oglala Lakota village. This night's

Fishing, Bears and Wolves

story telling has given the three braves a very high standing among all the villagers.

There are many young maidens in the village who have set their eyes upon the three young braves, even the short statured Ciqala, has a following among the young maidens, most especially and surprisingly so, a very tall one, with fine features of her long black hair and her eyes truly sparkle, whenever Ciqala catches her looking at him.

The attention given them, has not gone completely unnoticed by the young braves and they start to share stories among themselves whenever they are out hunting or fishing, each one claiming the attention of the fairest of the young Oglala Lakota maidens.

Each new brave laughing even harder as they make their stories bigger and funnier each time they are told. The most bragging stories told by each young brave, who repeatedly expands on their bravery and expresses, that they are not recognized properly among the other braves of their village, and that they deserve even more attention than they have received. All these stories become funnier with each expansion of the telling.

Mato Hota wakes early by the sounds of his mother, Winona (first born daughter), cooking the first meal of the day. "Good morning my mother," says Mato Hota.

Winona replies, "It will be so, when you eat, and then you go to bring me fresh fish. I am thinking of hogleglega (the grass pike, or the rainbow fish) in my cooking pot." "I will not return without a big rainbow trout or some of his smaller brothers," Mato Hota promises his mother. He eats hurriedly and bids his mother goodbye, as he gathers up his bow and fishing arrows, along with his spear, which he always carries.

Chief Matoskah had left days ago in search of a big pteoptaye (a buffalo herd), to bring meat for winter's coming snows. Winter will be cold and hard times will come, and much food will be needed to survive empty bellies occurring in the Oglala Lakota village.

Mato Hota, Luzahan and Ciqala, are walking up stream, heading for a small pool of slow-moving water where Mato Hota has previously seen a very large rainbow trout one day, while out hunting. He did not have his special wahinkpes (arrow) with wismahin (an arrowhead) with kestons (a barbed arrowhead) with him and would not waste any of his big game hunting arrows trying his luck shooting at the big ONE, he is after today.

The three braves reach the edge of the pool Mato Hota is leading them to, approaching slowly and quietly in their taha (deerskin) hanpa (moccasins). The big hogleglega is there and Mato Hota uses napeonwoglaka (sign language) to Luzahan and Ciqala, to be quiet, also informing them by signing that what he has been talking about is swimming slowly in a circle in the pool just below a big boulder near the pool's edge.

Mato Hota motions signing for Luzahan and Ciqala to stay still and he moves slowly to the backside of the boulder and climbs slowly and quietly up to the top and readies a keston wahinkpes in his bow. He slowly stands up and takes a step

Fishing, Bears and Wolves

forward and let's fly his wahinkpe at the big rainbow trout he is seeking. He barely misses, and he retrieves his arrow by pulling up his arrow by a thin piece of soft dried sintehanska (whitetail deer) takan (sinew) he took from his last deer hunt, which he has tied to his fishing wahinkpe before shooting at the big ONE.

The big trout slowly swims up stream out of the pool, turning his nose up at the fisherman and heads upstream toward some low flowing falls, completely out of range of any arrows. Maybe some bugs will come over the falls and he can eat them and grow even bigger.

Mato Hota and his brother braves search for fish for hours, but have no luck at finding any trout, even small ones to shoot their barbed arrows at. So far this fishing trip is not a campfire story to tell anyone, most especially Winona, Mato Hota's mother; it is a story so far without any standing at any campfire telling. Her smiling face may pucker up in a frowning manner, when he returns with empty hands, but with her, his dear mother, all is in a friendly manner.

The three 'great fishermen' make camp and build a campfire and tell stories of how they were lucky catching big fish on other fishing trips. Some were big enough to ride on according to Ciqala and that brought some laughter. As Luzahan tried to tell his fish story, he could not top Ciqala's story, unless he spoke of a swimming moose, which turned into a fish. However, this was not to be relevant on this day, as they came up empty handed.

However it was fun to be alive as new Oglala Lakota braves and to be one with nature's beauty among the tall pine trees fresh smell and to drink the clean water of the cold mountain stream, which they hunt by on many occasions, a true life's blood of their village. This night they must eat sintehanska jerky (smoked dried whitetail meat), which they carry when hunting and fishing in case neither yields a good outcome.

The three sleep soundly listening to nature's night sounds, some with the howling of wolves and barking of šunkmanitu (a coyote). Mato Ḣota is first to wake and is startled by the sight before him, it is a big hogleglega, —maybe his prized ONE, he has been fishing for— placed by the cold campfire, along with many more large rainbow trout. Mato Ḣota, kican (cries out loudly), "Up my brothers, we have company." Luzahan and Ciqala jump from their warm blankets grabbing their weapons and look around for something or someone to defend against, but see nothing threatening. Luzahan says, "What say you brother"? Mato Ḣota signs —points with the index finger of his right hand— toward the cold campfire and the big pile of rainbow trout. Luzahan says, "Who has brought hogleglega to us"?

The answer to Luzahan's question is soon answered as Mato Ḣota Titakuye (the grizzly bear - brother) of the braves begins to kapsanpsan, (sway to and fro) as he walks in with a big hogleglega in his mouth. Mato Ḣota Titakuye's appearance has

startled the three young braves. Mato Ḣota says, "Kanhtal

Fishing, Bears and Wolves

(relaxed, with a loss of tension), our bear bother has come in peace and friendship, to visit our camp and look what he has brought as a gift, many fresh hogleglega to take back to our village.

Let us eat some fresh fish and welcome our new brother Mato Ḣota Titakuye and share our gift of fine fresh hogleglega, given by waowešica (a bear, in general) brother, through Tatanka Ska Son's love for us, and brought to our almost campfire, which needs to be made by Ciqala."

Mato Ḣota and Luzahan start laughing and then to the surprise of the three young brave's, Mato Ḣota Titakuye opens his big mouth dropping his big fish and smiles and then, he too tries to laugh along with his new brothers, but instead he is h'eh'eya (slobbering) through his big lips, as if grinning. This causes even more laughter to break out. Oh, it is a good day to be an Oglala Lakota brave, with a giant brother from the woods to fish for you and share your campfire with fresh hogleglega to eat, what could be better?

Mato Ḣota roasts one of the bigger hogleglega over their campfire with a stick with the bark peeled off and stuck in its mouth and back to its tail fin. He offers some to Mato Ḣota Titakuye, but he shakes his big head with his mouth partly open and then eats some of the fresh catch of rainbow trout raw, as he always does and prefers that way. After a breakfast of hogleglega, all three braves give Mato Ḣota Titakuye a big hug, gather up the remaining fresh hogleglega, saving the biggest ONE for Winona, and head back to their village, with yet another incredible story to share at the campfires of all the villagers.

Mato Ḣota's mother, Winona, is very pleased with the fresh hogleglega, especially the big ONE he has brought to her. She gives her son a big hug and cheek rub with her soft right cheek. Most Indian mothers favor their sons more than their daughters, because their thoughts are of when they grow old and may become widows. They will need a hunter to feed them. That is why their sons are favored. But the daughters who help their mothers are loved no less, they may not be openly favored, but they are deeply loved no less.

The story of the great brown mato hota's gift of hogleglega, which he has gifted to Mato Hota, Luzahan and Ciqala, is received by many at campfires all around the village that night. Mato Hota's gift of mercy and kindness has brought the three young braves, a new bear brother, all thanks to Tatanka Ska Son, who made it so. No doubt in any one's closed mind, Tatanka Ska Son is watching over their three young brave brothers, and blessing them.

The three young Oglala Lakota braves have found themselves becoming great 'Story Tellers' and enjoy the telling, standing before many villagers, who hang on every word spoken by the three and they themselves, share these stories later again by many campfires through out their village. The three young braves are unaware that they are being trained, by these experiences, to be great 'Story Tellers', with many more to come, by no other than Tatanka Ska Son, the Wanikiye (the Savior).

Mato Hota's father, Chief Matoskah, mainly hunts tatanka (buffalo), so his son must hunt smaller game from the woods, to supply fresh meat for his mother and their tipi, while he is gone. When the hogleglega Mato Hota brought to his mother, Winona, has been eaten and most of the sintesapela (the black-tail or mule deer) jerky (smoked thins strips of venison - deer meat), is gone, Mato Hota gathers up his brother braves, Luzahan and Ciqala

Fishing, Bears and Wolves

and they head out into the deep forest of tall pines, spruce and fir, in search of sintehanska (whitetail deer) or sintesapela or maybe, if they are very blessed, a big bull hehaka (the male elk). The hehaka meat tastes much better than tahca (the common deer), but the braves will be thankful for anything the Great Spirit, Wakantanka, will allow them to harvest.

As the three young braves are trailing through the tall trees, spread out about forty feet apart to increase their chances of seeing game. They are miles from their village and have had no hunting success all day, although they did spot a small sintehanska, but unbeknown to them, a big sintesapela (the black-tail or mule deer), saw them first and ran away with his black-tail popping up and down, just as if he was waving goodbye with a big smile on his face, as he ran up the mountain side, as the braves were approaching his location.

Sunset is calling a halt to their hunt and the three braves make camp by a big boulder and are just about to start a campfire, when they hear the cry of wolves close by them. Mato Hota yells, "Šungmanitu (a wolf), climb up the boulder katka (briskly)." Ciqala, is having trouble climbing up the boulder and Luzahan pulls him up, just in time, as a big gray šungmanitu tanka (big wolf) probably weighing around two hundred and fifty pounds, clamps his mouth shut, just missing Ciqala's left foot, by a hair's width. The šungmanitu tanka lands on the ground and lets out a big howl, soon a very large pack of hungry šungmanitus run in to join their leader and surround the three young braves on top of the huge boulder.

All thanks goes to Wakantanka, who must have planned their camping site without their knowledge, having them choose this place by this huge boulder, which they were fortunate enough to have chosen to camp by with His untold guidance.

Mato Hota pulls a hunting arrow from his wanju (an arrow pouch or a quiver), and places it in his bow, looking at the šungmanitu leader, he pulls his bow string back as far as he can stretch it, keeping the wismahin (arrowhead) close to his stretched-out left arm and hand. He quickly aims, lets his arrow go and it flies and hits the tanka šungmanitu leader, but only nicks him in his left hip. The šungmanitu leader lets out a cry of pain and quickly moves away into the trees, but not before Luzahan, has made a killing shot with his bow and arrow on another large male wolf, who screams as he falls off his feet and life slips from him forever and he will hunt no more with his pack brothers and sisters on Mother Earth.

Darkness has made it hard to see the šungmanitu pack, as they settle down in the trees to wait out the three young braves, who must come down eventually to get water. This šungmanitu leader is wise and knows how to hunt his prey. It is a cold night the three young braves must spend it on top of the huge boulder, but they are thankful for its cold oiputake (kiss) to their feet, as it offers safety and a comfortable refuge and shelter from the large šungmanitu pack. Mato Hota guesses, that there must be more than twenty šungmanitus, a very large pack, for sure.

Mato Hota yells, "Count your arrows, how many do you have"? Luzahan answers, "I have only two, as I like to use my spear." Ciqala speaks up, "I have five my brother and my wicat'e (an instrument with which to kill) to use." Mato Hota speaks out seriously, "We have nine wahinkpes with my two hunting wahinkpes left and that may not be enough to save us from the whole šungmanitu pack. Maybe if we can kill many of the most embolden and brave of the wolves, the others will leave us and return to the forest."

After a long cold night of worrying and watching for attacking wolves, the three are silently waiting for action, ready to fight with courage for their lives against the huge numbers of gray šungmanitu, as dawn is breaking.

Luzahan, sees that the šungmanitu he shot with his hunting arrow the night before is no longer visible, "My šungmanitu, who carries my arrow in his neck, is gone, the rest of šungmanitu pack must have eaten him. Remember hearing the loud growls and noise of fighting in the middle of the dark night? These šungmanitu are very hungry, and hunger makes for much bravery," says Luzahan.

Mato Hota states firmly, "They will come soon, be ready with your arrows as dawn slips away to morning light. Be sure to wait and be wantanyeya (be skillful in shooting) with first light, we must take many, and maybe the others will go far away, so we can run away to the river, where if they come upon us again, we can crush their skulls with our wicat'es as they swim toward us." Ciqala asks, "When our arrows are gone, we must fight them with our wicat'es and spears for stabbing them."

Mato Hota pauses and then speaks up again, "When our arrows are gone, and more enemy šungmanitu have been taken, we will wait them out here on this big rock my brothers." Ciqala states, "It is a good plan, I can wait, until our water is gone and then some, before I climb down." This brings a low sounding laugh from all the young braves, building up their nerve again as new warrior braves.

The lead šungmanitu of the pack sends in his strongest brothers to circle the boulder and try to run up the backside.

Mato Hota is waiting for the first one to try and climb up and his arrow finds it mark. The šungmanitu lets out a loud scream and falls to the ground and goes still, as life swiftly leaves him. Three more šungmanitus attack at the same time and get half way up the front side of the boulder facing the sun, it is a little hard to see, as the sun is coming in bright through the surrounding trees, but three more arrows find their mark as Mato Hota, Luzahan and Ciqala, shoot at the same time. Five arrows are all that stand between the wolf pack and the three young braves being forced to fight on the ground, when their water is gone.

Four šungmanitus attack from behind the boulder and the three braves barely have time to shoot their bows again, three go down, but one gets footing and comes up to attack Ciqala who is closest. It is a big mistake for him, Ciqala swings his wicat'e hard in a downward loop and hits the šungmanitu in the head and he yelps, before his limp body slides down the big boulder. Mato Hota says loudly, "Good kill Ciqala, good warrior now."

Two arrows are all the young braves have left. Mato Hota speaks up, "Ciqala you have one arrow and Luzahan, all yours have found their mark. Ciqala give your last arrow to Luzahan and use your wicat'e at the rear of our big brother rock, to keep us safe, as you just did. Luzahan and I will watch from the front and sides, Luzahan you can take the next one who attacks closest to you with Ciqala's last arrow. I am going to wait for the šungmanitu leader to come close enough for my arrow to find his evil heart."

The two braves nod in agreement of Mato Hota's words. Luzahan answers, "It is a good plan, if you take his life maybe his brother šungmanitus will leave us." The entire remaining šungmanitu pack has pulled back into the trees waiting for their leader to lead them in another attack or leave this hard hunt, to hunt for easier prey. They will follow him, whatever his choice may be or face his wrath. The šungmanitu brothers are howling in low tones, as their leader lets out a long loud howl. It is his signal to the pack to all rush in on the three young braves.

Luzahan takes down a big gray šungmanitu running beside the leader with his last arrow. Mato Hota is waiting for the wolf leader to run in closer to shoot his last arrow at his heart. As šungmanitu leader closes in, Mato Hota shoots his arrow and it hits the big šungmanitu in his upper left front leg and he goes down howling in pain.

Just then out of nowhere Mato Hota Titakuye (Grizzly Brother) runs in between the attacking šungmanitu and the big brother rock, Mato Hota, Luzahan and Ciqala are standing on. Mato Hota Titakuye swats the first two big šungmanitus, who do not stop charging, sending them flying away into the bushes and among the trees, howling in pain.

Mato Hota Titakuye's next move is over to the big wounded šungmanitu leader, and he places his huge right paw on his neck and is just about to bite him in the chest with his big strong jaws agape showing a mouth full of big sharp teeth bared from his loose lips, when a bright blue light containing Tatanka Ska Son appears and He says, "Hold now Mato Hota Titakuye, do not kill this šungmanitu leader, I have need of him."

The great brown mato hota immediately removes his great paw from the neck of the šungmanitu leader and sits down on his haunches in total stillness. Tatanka Ska Son requests in a calm manner, "Come down from the rock Mato Hota, I need your healing powers." Mato Hota slides down from his high perch and rushes to face Tatanka Ska Son and kneels before him. Tatanka Ska Son instructs Mato Hota, "Cut in deep with your hunting knife and free the arrow head in the šungmanitu leader's leg and pull it out, he will not bite you."

Mato Hota approaches the šungmanitu leader with some caution, and slowly kneels beside the big šungmanitu leader, who is in pain and panting rapidly, but lying very still. The wounded wolf leader raises his head, looking at Mato Hota, and does not move as he gently lifts his front leg up. Mato Hota takes out his flint hunting knife and cuts into the leader's upper left leg, next to the arrowhead and cuts it free of leg muscle, grabs the arrow shaft firmly, then he slowly pulls it out of the big šungmanitu leader's leg, whose gray eyes have been constantly fixed on and intently looking at Tatanka Ska Son, not Mato Hota who has been cutting on him.

The šungmanitu leader seems to be in a trance and unaware of any pain. He is lying perfectly still and remains totally quiet, showing no pain from the cutting and removing of Mato Hota's hunting arrow from his wounded left leg near his shoulder. Mato Hota washes the wound of the wolf leader with water from his almost empty water pouch, and to his amazement, the wound instantly disappears with no trace of his injury remaining visible.

"Mato Hota, speak to your new brother Šungmanitu Aitancan (wolf ruler) over all other wolf packs, within your lands. Speak to him with sign language and he will understand and be your new brother, for he is healed by your hand through My Father, Wakantanka. You, Mato Hota, are to be known from this day forward, as Okiziwakiya (the healer). You have the power of healing, whenever you call on My Father for this healing power, it will be granted to you, as it has been now, as you healed this

Fishing, Bears and Wolves

šungmanitu before you. You will be honored among all who know you from this day until you join My Father in Mahpiya (Heaven). Šungmanitu (a wolf) Aitancan (ruler), 'Wolf Ruler' is healed, he will follow you in peace to your village and all will honor you and by his presence alone, they will believe My Story given to you this day. I, Tatanka Ska Son have spoken."

Okiziwakiya is overwhelmed with this new power and new name of honor given to him and speaks in appreciation to Tatanka Ska Son, "I will do my people all good in Your Name and that of The Great Father, Wakantanka, God, the Creator of all, that is. I will serve you always." Tatanka Ska Son speaks again, "You, Luzahan and Ciqala, have learned today, that even an enemy can become a brother through mercy, kindness and the showing of love." Tatanka Ska Son, nods to the big gray šungmanitu ruler, who also hears and understands the words Tatanka Ska Son has spoken to his new brother brave of the Oglala Lakota band. Saving lives, healing and 'Story Telling' are finished and Tatanka Ska Son lifts off and disappears into the sky above, straight into the early day's bright sunlight.

Luzahan and Ciqala are beaming with happiness —not to mention being saved from the wolf pack of many numbers— and with new pride because of the new powers given to their brother. His new name of honor, Okiziwakiya, which is only given as a brave, becomes known by a new name earned by deed or misdeed, as the case may be. The šungmanitu pack gather around Šungmanitu Aitancan, their new 'wolf ruler', who has been healed and lick him and nuzzle him in a show of respect and submission and acts of affection to their powerful new ruler given new power by Tatanka Ska Son, along with his gift of new human friends, the three young Oglala Lakota braves.

The Chosen Ones Oglala Warriors

Okiziwakiya, Luzahan and Ciqala move off toward the village with a new friendly šungmanitu pack following close behind, now many brothers of the woods. No game has been taken yet on this hunting trip, but the day is not yet over.

Okiziwakiya makes a kill of a big buck sintesapela with his spear, now he has meat for his tipi, as well as many new animal friends. He can hardly wait to enter the village with this new army of strange friends from the forest following along with him. Just before reaching his village, he kneels and prays, "Thank you Wakantanka, for Your blessing and the gift of life, which I dedicate to Your Will."

As the young hunters all near the Oglala Lakota village, Okiziwakiya will warn the first village outer guard he encounters and tell him his animal friends come in peace. However, that time has not yet come and will be told in another Oglala Lakota Indian story in the next Campfire Story Telling – "The Earlier Earth and Mother Earth." Until then, Wakantanka's Blessings will flow upon those who believe in Him, let that Blessing be on you.

Sintesapela (black-tail deer or mule deer)

Chapter 6

The Earlier Earth and Mother Earth

Okiziwakiya (to cause to heal up) is leading his brothers Luzahan (swift) and Ciqala (little one) through tall, tightly packed pine trees on his way back to their village. No longer empty handed in this hunt, he is excited to get back to his village and tell the story he and his brothers have just lived. Walking beside Okiziwakiya at his left hand is Šungmanitu (a wolf) Aitancan (the ruler over), his new šungmanitu brother Wolf Ruler, followed by his šungmanitu pack, who are walking behind the leader in single file. Suddenly, Šungmanitu Aitancan bolts off through the forest heading toward the nearby mountain stream the three young Oglala (to scatter one's own) Lakota (the Siouan people) braves often fish in and travel by. Šungmanitu Aitancan has spotted two large heȟaka (the male elk) and makes a wolf call signal with his tail wagging in a circle. This is his command signaling for his pack to come and split off and surround the two big buck elk. It is a successful hunt and the pack begins feeding on one of the heȟaka, as they are all very hungry. Šungmanitu Aitancan guards the other elk and lets the pack know that this one is his alone.

Šungmanitu Aitancan runs back to find Okiziwakiya and his brothers, Luzahan and Ciqala and leads them to the hunting spot where his big heȟaka is left untouched, except for one bite to the neck from his strong jaws. Šungmanitu Aitancan runs around Okiziwakiya circling several times, and then he goes to the big elk and circles him many times. He is speaking in napeonwoglaka (sign language) to Okiziwakiya, indicating he is giving his hunting prize to Okiziwakiya and his new Oglala Lakota brothers. It is his way to show his gift of heȟaka is meant in thanks and friendship for saving his life and healing his wounded leg, and most important being new brothers of the two legs.

Now, they have more meat than they can carry and put all the elk meat on the backs of the wolves to carry, strapping the elk meat on their backs with strips of hide from the elk.

When Okiziwakiya, Luzahan and Ciqala, enter the edge of their village after having passed by the village guard, each villager who sees them is frozen in place in amazement and wonder at what they see with their very own eyes. It is unbelievable, but true. Okiziwakiya is shouldering a large pole on each shoulder loaded with sintesapela meat and Luzahan is at the back end of one of the poles carrying this end of the pole,

The Earlier Earth and Mother Earth

with Ciqala helping with the load on the end of the opposite pole, next to Luzahan. What they see is much more, Šungmanitu Aitancan is walking on the left side of Okiziwakiya and the entire wolf pack is following their leader in single file according to their standing in their šungmanitu pack carrying elk meat on their backs.

It is a sight never before seen by the Oglala Lakota before this special time in the history of their tribe. The braves carry the sintesapela meat to the chief's tipi (teepee or tent or lodge) and stop at the door, letting their heavy load gently to the ground. Chief Matoskah (white bear) has returned from his successful hunt of tatanka (buffalo) and hears the noises outside his tipi and comes out to greet the three young hunters. The three hunters stand tall after laying their sintesapela meat down.

Okiziwakiya speaks up, "My father, it is my honor to bring you this gift of sintesapela and hehaka meat, but most of all to bring you and our brothers of the village, our new friend Šungmanitu Aitancan, ruler of this gray šungmanitu pack and all wolf packs in our lands. Their leader, Šungmanitu Aitancan, you see here by my side, killed the big hehaka and gifted him to me. If that not be so, I would be less empty handed in our hunt." Chief Matoskah is very impressed by what he has heard from his son, Mato Hota (grizzly bear) —the name given him at birth— and now sees the fresh hehaka meat before his very own eyes in the fullness of the sunlight carried by all the wolf pack.

Chief Matoskah, "This is a day of yuonihan (to honor, treat

with attention, politeness) we must prepare our gift of elk meat and share with our new brother Šungmanitu Aitancan and from this day, all Oglala Lakota will treat these new šungmanitu brothers with kindness and always be canteyukan (to have a heart, to be benevolent) generous in sharing food, wherever we find them in need. They will always be welcome in our village. Women of the village prepare the meat and cooking fires. We will dance the Wiwanyank Wacipi (the Sundance) this night. Mato Hota, Luzahan and Ciqala come into my lodge, each tell story!"

The three braves tell their stories to Chief Matoskah, making wayahloka (to persuade, to make an impression talking) to their great chief, and he has heard their words clearly and taken them to heart. Luzahan has spoken up about Tatanka Ska Son (Son of Wakantanka) giving Mato Hota his second name, that being Okiziwakiya and this is taken as great news by Chief Matoskah knowing his son will be a blessing for the Oglala Lakota people. This means Tatanka Ska Son has given the tribe a 'Healer', and that Tatanka Ska Son, loves and honors all the Oglala Lakota people with the giving of this most valuable gift. This is truly a wonderful gift and the great chief is feeling great respect for his son.

The village women do as Chief Matoskah has commanded and all is prepared. The three braves are greeted by the other braves who consider Mato Hota to be wakanyan (one who does wonderful things). He is truly becoming one to honor among his people.

All the villagers are eating the sintesapela and hehaka brought to them by Mato Hota and his wolf ruler (šungmanitu aitancan) brother of the woods. The women have cooked the sintesapela and hehaka meat on the cooking fires and many have

The Earlier Earth and Mother Earth

eaten, some have begun to dance and sing in joy and harmony. Mato Hota is seated on the right of his father, Chief Matoskah, and lying beside him, is Šungmanitu Aitancan, who has a full belly and is calmly watching the dancing of the Oglala Lakota people with his big gray eyes reflecting the campfire nearby.

Two of Šungmanitu Aitancan's pack have taken up with Luzahan and Ciqala, who are rubbing their muzzles and petting them as they lay quietly by their side around a big campfire. The women and young maidens are seated behind the men and some are starting to dance scattered in among the braves.

Chief Matoskah stands up slowly and all goes silent among all villagers. The chief speaks in a loud voice, "Today is a special day of haho haho (express of joy on receiving something). Today Mato Hota, my son, has brought Šungmanitu Aitancan to our village and he has given us a gift of the hehaka and he and his pack are to be known as a takuya (to have one for a relation). I have learned today Tatanka Ska Son has visited my son and given new powers of healing and a new name to Mato Hota. He is to be known as Okiziwakiya from this day forward. It is a good day for our Oglala Lakota people and that is all I have to say!" The great chief hugs his son and sits down to eat again, as the food is very tasty and he is ready for elk meat, since he has been eating buffalo for weeks.

Many braves come to honor Okiziwakiya. After all braves have congratulated him, a young maiden he has been watching with interest, and who has been looking at young Okiziwakiya with the light of the stars in her eyes, finds even more admiration for him after hearing his new name and what it means among her tribal members.

A slight breeze blows its cool fresh smelling air in her long black soft wisp of hair, as she sits by a campfire, also not going unnoticed by other braves. Okiziwakiya looks her way and catches her staring at him with her beautiful face beaming in the light of the campfire, showing a sheepish smile on her young face.

She seems a little embarrassed by her boldness shown toward him, as she is only in the early thirteenth season of life, but she cannot help herself, for she holds deep love secretly in her heart for Okiziwakiya. He nods slightly in a return of her kind gesture toward him, not wanting to embarrass her among those watching their every move.

She is called Wachiwi (dancing girl) and he has seen her dance and her dance is graceful, like the white swan swimming smoothly through the water on a calm lake. When she dances, she leaves ripples of meaning in her smooth flowing motions, behind each movement she creates to the beat of drums and song meanings. To see her move now as she gets up and begins to dance slowly, reminds him of the thoughts he has carried in his mind of her when she is out of his sight. Sometimes, he must clear his thoughts of her beautiful face, to concentrate on his hunting skills, lest his arrows go astray, not finding its target when he is hunting.

This is hard for him to do and it troubles Okiziwakiya, for he is expecting much from himself, as he becomes a fully grown brave and warrior brother to Tatanka Ska Son, the Son of Wakantanka (The Great Spirit, the Creator, God). Much has been

The Earlier Earth and Mother Earth

given and much is expected, at least in his mind. His heart tells him this story louder each day.

Okiziwakiya tells Luzahan and Ciqala while sitting at their campfire on another hunt, "In Oglala Lakota life, one is recognized by a new name each time he has reached a certain level of respect or dishonor, either by good deeds or by evil deeds committed by that person and they will be known by that name, until it changes again or rides him or her, like a horse forever into the sunset.

"Tatanka Ska Son knows us by the name we earn, mine is now Okiziwakiya, known only by the Oglala Lakota people. Chief Bagwungijik (hole in the sky) of the Chippewa (Anishináabe meaning 'original person') may also earn a new name if that is the wish of his Chippewa people, which I do not know if this custom is part of their ways. This way of the Oglala Lakota is a good way, because it keeps one in honor or disrespect, as each one earns his way in the honor or dishonor of life. It is much better to be known and called by a good new name of honor, than to be held in disrespect and called by that name by all the people of the Oglala Lakota Nation.

"I say, with words in your thoughts, how do you want to be called by Tatanka Ska Son or as some say, the Great Mystery, and The Great Spirit, the Creator, God, Wakantanka, when you meet Them or when you enter Their thoughts as They watch over you? That is the thinking of Okiziwakiya and my words of council, mind your thoughts, for they can be good or evil and Wakantanka can read their sign."

Luzahan and Ciqala nod in agreement to Okiziwakiya, for his words are wise beyond his young years. They discuss the names they wish to be known by often, while enjoying their hunting and fishing campfires. Each young brave is in complete agreement, they do not want to be known by an evil or dishonorable name and pledge to each other as brothers and to Tatanka Ska Son in prayer, that it will always be so. For now, Luzahan and Ciqala are known by the names they now hold among the Oglala Lakota villagers.

The next day, Okiziwakiya is in his family tipi and has just finished his noon meal cooked by his mother, when he is shaken from his thoughts of Wachiwi, which are weighing heavy on his

mind as a young teenager feeling new unfamiliar emotions, by a middle aged brave who has run hard and fast to find him. His name is Wanhi (flint) and he tells Okiziwakiya in an urgent voice, that his little daughter Zonta (honest, trustworthy) has fallen in the cold water of the swift mountain stream while gathering water. He has pulled her out, but she was cold and unconscious when he pulled her from the swift waters. Okiziwakiya follows Wanhi at a run, to the side of Zonta, who is lying on her side and is very still and lifeless.

Okiziwakiya kneels by Zonta's side and calls on Wakantanka for help, "Oh Great One, Wakantanka, help me to bring back life into Zonta, she needs Our help." Wakantanka speaks only to Okiziwakiya in his mind, but as clear as if He was speaking to

The Earlier Earth and Mother Earth

him in a voice to be heard by one's ear. Wakantanka speaks silently only to Okiziwakiya's mind saying, 'Okiziwakiya hear Me now, slowly turn Zonta over on her back and push on the center of her chest with both hands, one on top of the other. Do this in short time beats like the drum between each push; keep the rhythm until she is breathing on her own strength'.

Okiziwakiya does as he is instructed by Wakantanka. Soon, Zonta coughs up a mouth full of water and she comes to life again and begins to cry softly and whimper. Okiziwakiya tells her, "Do not cry my little sister, you are safe and your father has saved you from the cold waters."

Wanhi interrupts in a soft voice and corrects Okiziwakiya, "It is you who have saved my winona (first born daughter) Zonta, my heart and service in this life are yours, you are my strong friend for all time." Okiziwakiya responds, "Give thanks to Wakantanka, for His hand alone has restored your precious Zonta to your tipi; He only used me to help as His hand on Mother Earth."

All the villagers are amazed by the saving of Zonta by Okiziwakiya and this story of healing is told throughout the village by her father, Wanhi's story telling. Many are filled with the feeling of igluwankatuya (to elevate or raise up one's self, over others; i.e. to be proud), being filled with pride, at the thought of having such a brother for their very own among their

Oglala Lakota village. Okiziwakiya is now truly a healer and their Oglala Lakota village now has their very own 'healer' to help them when in need of healing and sometimes restore them to life. It is a great blessing from

Wakantanka.

Chief Matoskah is keenly aware of the new powers of his son, through his being chosen as a brother to Tatanka Ska Son and given special powers to help his people and his pride is above all others. For he surely knows, that his son will someday be Chief of his Oglala Lakota people, when he "walks on" to Mahpiya (Heaven). Even so, he is troubled and does not understand this great mystery. For now, he will place this mystery away and trust in Tatanka Ska Son.

Okiziwakiya is walking alone beside the mountain stream near his village and is listening to the rapids whispering its love song of contentment, through its sound to his ears coming directly from Mother Earth's goodness. It is good for him to be alive in this time and listen to her song. Okiziwakiya is full of hope, as he walks peacefully and he is very content with his life. He is thinking he is alone, but Tatanka Ska Son is silently walking unseen by his side. As he makes his way around a large boulder, he sees Tatanka Ska Son now standing before him, waiting to talk to him face to face.

Okiziwakiya quickly kneels in a show of reverence and respect, to Tatanka Ska Son. "Stand up My brother; I have come to tell you a story My Father wants Me to pass on to you. The great story, the Creator, God wants you to pass on to your Oglala tribe and all the Lakota Nation and any others you may wish to tell. Sit down upon the soft pine needles I have gathered for your comfort My brother and I will tell you of how your people came to Mother Earth. From now on I will teach you and your brothers who believe in Me and My Father, Wakantanka,

The Earlier Earth and Mother Earth

God, the Creator of all." Okiziwakiya moves to the pine needle seat prepared for him to sit on.

"Long, long, long, ago in the most tannika (old, worn out) 'ancient' of times, a time before this earth or it's moon, where set among the stars to fly freely around the great wi (sun), which warms and feeds Mother Earth with her light, there was another Earlier Earth. The Earlier Earth was created far away from here, among many stars.

"The Creator who has always been, is now and will forever be, is all powerful, however powerful, He became lonely and He had no children or family to love and care for. He had no brothers or sisters to watch over, as you do now. When the Creator, God, Wakantanka, made this world, He put upon it many animals, trees and plants, He made the rivers to run clear and the oceans of varying tolahcaka (very blue) colors were filled with many living creatures.

"It was a wondrous place filled with an abundance of life in many forms. He created one people to live upon this Earlier Earth, which He created before the Mother Earth you live upon now. He gave them complete freedom to rule themselves without any laws or customs to follow, because He loved them unconditionally as His very own children.

"My Father did not want to command them to love Him, for that kind of love would have no value or meaning. He wanted their love to be given freely to Him from their hearts, and for them to worship Him as their Creator and God. He had only one law that they must follow. That law was not to eat from the 'Tree of Knowledge', which He put in the middle of a lush meadow. He did not want them to eat of this tree, because He wanted them to come to Him for knowledge. So, He commanded them not to eat of that tree.

"Wakantanka had provided many other fruits and vegetables for them to eat and they had a life of plenty to live upon. All the animals were their friends among this wonderment, until there was a trickster born among them as a snake and this snake could talk, and he could do wakan'econpila (magic, tricks of jugglery), and he deceived them, and turned them from the love of their Father God, known to you as Wakantanka, The Great Spirit, the Creator, God.

"The trickster gathered the humans there around the 'Tree of Knowledge' in the lush meadow and said to them in a boisterous voice, 'Watch me eat of the "Tree of Knowledge" and no harm will come to me.'

"The people believed him and also, ate of the "Tree of Knowledge" after the trickster had eaten of the forbidden tree and they saw no harm had come to him. Now they disobeyed Wakantanka's one law and all sinned against God and ate of the 'Tree of Knowledge'. After all His children betrayed Him and they had eaten the forbidden fruit from the 'Tree of Knowledge', all went dark.

"The Creator in great sorrow, turned His Face from them and sent the Earlier Earth's sun away from them and all life was swallowed into great darkness and the crippling grip of cold, all life to be no more. Wakantanka destroyed this Earlier Earth He had created, turning it into many pieces of hard black stone, harder than any known stone on this Mother Earth. He sent all these black stones grouped together, spinning like a cyclone, far away among the stars to crash in total destruction of all the beauty He had created for them, into the powerful gravity suction

The Earlier Earth and Mother Earth

of a gigantic black hole and Earlier Earth was gobbled up like a fish in a hungry mato hota's big mouth."

Tatanka Ska Son pauses and then begins speaking again, "After ehanna (long ago) in the universe which He created, before even giving birth to the countless stars you may understand by watching a night sky high above. Wakantanka, The Great Spirit, the Creator, God, once again grew lonely and desired to create human beings once again in the likeness of Himself and put them upon your present new Mother Earth. He would make this new earth with His wish for all things to serve each other and Him only. All they had to do was believe in Him and His Son, Me, Tatanka Ska Son.

"He started His creation with huge creatures in the beginning to roam Mother Earth. Big gigantic plant eaters, who ate in the tops of tall trees and some tanka (large, great in any way) meat eaters to hold the plant eater' numbers down, but they proved to be much too dangerous for His human beings to live with in harmony, so Wakantanka sent a huge arrow of fire from the sky and destroyed all the huge fearsome creatures, giant lizards with huge teeth, cold blooded killers, that could not get along with the new children He would create.

"He let Mother Earth heal from her wounds for many, many moons, before He would place upon her a man and He would take a rib from that man and create a companion in the form of a woman, so the man would not be alone on Mother Earth and know loneliness as He had suffered.

"He also, created the animals you hunt today and those that have a purpose in the replenishment of her healthy blaya (level, plain) "balance" in nature. The animals would eat the plants and leaves, some animals would serve by giving their life on Mother

Earth to feed others —man and meat eating beast— and they would join Him in Mahpiya, all healed and whole as in life before death, as all living things do without exception, but for one. All this wonder of Mother Earth He created in six days, a small part of one full moon in time.

"The one which would not be joining Him upon their death would be the human beings, for they had been evil on the Earlier Earth and betrayed Him. This time, He would require human beings to believe in Him, and His Son, Me, which He has sent at this time, to teach all who will listen of God's new laws and to follow His laws and the customs the Oglala Lakota people live by. These customs which are that of the Oglala Lakota people, which He has taught your forefathers through good living lessons in the balance of using Mother Earth's gifts wisely.

"He has chosen your people many, many moons ago, when He created them to live on the new earth, Mother Earth. He gave them your customs of respect for all things, which they passed down in story telling at many campfires. Telling all, that things of Mother Earth are to be treated as a living thing and for all to treat them with respect and love, for they serve mankind His children.

"This is your Oglala Lakota custom and it is a good custom, passed to them by Wakantanka. You must teach all of these customs to all future humans, but most of all, you must teach all people to believe in My Father, Wakantanka, The Great Spirit, the Creator, God and Me, Tatanka Ska Son, as His Son, your Teacher and Brother. Okiziwakiya, this is your mission as My brother and that mission is to be your journey in this life, for you have been chosen by Wakantanka to be a 'Chosen One'. That is all I have to say this day."

The Earlier Earth and Mother Earth

Tatanka Ska Son flies away into the sun, leaving Okiziwakiya, who is stunned by this greatest of stories and by the great honor to be the 'Chosen One' to share it with all who will listen, and to tell future stories, which his Wakan Teacher, Tatanka Ska Son, has given him to share, as a most special and blessed "Chosen One."

Okiziwakiya is completely over come with the thought of Tatanka Ska Son's Words, and remains seated on the ground atop the seat of pine needles, for a long time deep into the night. He has been thinking of what he has been told by Tatanka Ska Son and putting into his mind the Words spoken by Tatanka Ska Son, before returning to his village.

Okiziwakiya has been planning to tell this great story from Tatanka Ska Son, with all details of the story of the beginning of time of this world Mother Earth and the other Earlier Earth, which He destroyed. Tatanka Ska Son placed all the Words He had spoken in the mind of Okiziwakiya, just as He spoke them. All Oglala and all Lakota people must hear this story and nothing must be allowed iglasto (to be left out, incomplete) of Tatanka Ska Son's Wakan (sacred, holy) Words spoken to him this day.

Until the next Campfire Story Telling - "A Young Woman's Dance and a Brave Rescue," is shared, may Wakantanka Bless You, as you tell His stories by your campfire or on the trail of life.

Lakota Chief Red Cloud

Chapter 7

A Young Woman's Dance and A Brave Rescue

When Okiziwakiya (to cause to heal up) returns to his village the ceremonial wiyatapika wacipi (dancing, a dance), the coming of age of a girl, to a young maiden, is being held for none other than Wachiwi (dancing girl), whom he admires greatly. This is a time when a young girl is changing in life to a child bearing woman, a most sacred time in one's life as a girl among her tribe. This ceremony is to be held in order to purify her in preparation to become a maiden and to be known among all the villagers as a young girl, reaching the status of a woman. Her family built a tipi (teepee or tent or lodge) and gathered all the necessary items required for the ritual.

The ritual will be performed by the old medicine man Takoda (friend to everyone). Okiziwakiya smells the sweetgrass burning and sees all ceremonial objects being purified by the smoke Takoda has prepared. Next, the pipe is smoked and a prayer is spoken by Takoda, the Medicine man, offered up to Wakantanka (The Great Spirit, the Creator, God) in the four directions of the earth, as is the custom of the Oglala (to scatter one's own) Lakota (the Siouan people).

Continuing in the ceremony, a buffalo skull —a central important object— which is covered with red paint to symbolize Mother Earth, has cherries and fresh water placed before it. Then tobacco is spread out in the shape of a cross, which is then painted blue and put on display to represent the coming together of Mother Earth and the sky.

Okiziwakiya watches with great respect seeing Wachiwi dressed, wearing huiyakaskes (ankle ornaments for the Sundance), a kangiha mignaka (a feather disk), resembling the unhcela kagapi (a fixed bustle to the rear), which is a bustle used in dancing and having a center-like to that of the mescal bean in the upper flower-like part, along with kangiha mignaka, becoming a feather ornament fastened on the back and dangling down. It is also worn in the Omaha Dance, a peša (Omaha headgear), a ptehe wapaha (horned headgear), an unhcela kagapi, a wacinhin (a headdress), a wacinhin sapsapa (black plumes), a wacinhinya (to use for a plume), and a wapaha hetonpi (a horned

A Young Woman's Dance and A Brave Rescue

headdress). Wachiwi appears wearing all, which are stunningly beautiful to him.

The ceremony continues when Wachiwi is given a piece of buffalo meat by Takoda, who also passes the water and cherries to members of her family. This is the completion by Takoda the 'Medicine Man' for the Oglala Lakota in this small village.

After this part of the ceremony has been completed, a feast is held and many small gifts are given away to all villagers by the family of Wachiwi. Now, the goodness and holiness that has come to this young girl Wachiwi, is also then extended to the entire tribe. Okiziwakiya is happy for Wachiwi and when she catches his eyes looking at her, she beams him a big smile to cross the distance between them. It is a good time in the Oglala Lakota village this day.

Okiziwakiya is able to offer congratulations to Wachiwi, along with a big smile, which is taken as a special gift by Wachiwi, who has her eyes on him and cantekiya (to love, to have an affection for) in her heart for this special brave with great standing among her Oglala Lakota village.

After honoring Wachiwi, he goes to his father and mother's tipi, to practice his story told by Tatanka Ska Son, while his mother and father are still celebrating Wachiwi's coming of age as a young maiden. He must tell this great story of Earlier Earth and Mother Earth's creation told to him by Tatanka Ska Son. A story soon to be told to all the villagers by campfire that they may know the Words Tatanka Ska Son has shared with him about Wakantanka and His creation of Mother Earth. But he must share this with his father, Chief Matoskah (white bear), first and have his blessing to speak to the entire village of Oglala Lakota.

Chief Matoskah, after having heard all Okiziwakiya has told him, calls all the band of Oglala Lakota to a giant campfire the following night and calls on Okiziwakiya, his fine son to speak to the people with his blessing of his words to be spoken. Okiziwakiya asks all in the village to listen closely to his words, as they have been told to him by Tatanka Ska Son, which Wakan (Holy) Tatanka Ska Son has directed him to tell all who will listen.

The entire village is totally silent and waits to hear Okiziwakiya's words spoken to him from Tatanka Ska Son and when he has finished telling his greatest of campfire stories, there is much talk among the villagers. Many words are shared, long after the great campfire has gone low. These words from Tatanka Ska Son, shared by Okiziwakiya, have made yuajaja (to explain, to make clear e.g. a doctrine) many mysteries held by the villagers before this greatest of campfire story telling they have ever heard or has ever been passed down through the ages by their ancestors in all previous 'campfire story telling'.

It is a great new day in the Oglala Lakota village. A day of great joy has been shared by all in the Oglala Lakota village. Each villager realizing, that all they have to do, to go to Mahpiya (Heaven), is believe in Wakantanka and His Son, Tatanka Ska Son, and love all His children.

Chief Matoskah has been thinking of the power and the greatness of his son has achieved, by being the brother of Tatanka Ska Son and all Okiziwakiya has done for the Oglala Lakota village. He has decided his son must take a third new name. He has decided that the name will be wanagiyata (in the land of spirits) yet to become famous to the Oglala Lakota people for all time to come. He will give his son his new name

A Young Woman's Dance and A Brave Rescue

Wanagiyata before the Council of Elders and then the entire village within a sunrise.

That will have to wait, for Okiziwakiya, Luzahan and Ciqala have slipped out of the village to hunt and have made big plans to bring more buffalo meat to the village, for their goal in life is to always earn the respect of the Oglala Lakota people. They have taken three horses for riding and three for hauling any buffalo meat they feel sure to bring back after a good hunt. Okiziwakiya as a boy has overheard talk of the tribal elders, stories of many tatanka (buffalo), many days ride from the Oglala Lakota village on horseback, over mountains in the southwest, very near the Crow (Apsáalooke – children of the large-beaked bird – Siouan language) people, previously coming from the Yellow Stone River area.

These stories presented a challenge to the new young braves and they must find out if any of the stories were true. If they were true, they could have a very successful hunt and if not, it would still be a great adventure and opportunity to tell stories at many campfires. They told no one that they were going to this far away place. After all, they are new Oglala Lakota braves and believe their actions should not be questioned by those suffering with the curse of long nose and many more, showing long in the tooth when speaking words with no value!

The three traveled through some rough country and many times were forced to walk and guide their horses up and down and around mountainous terrain. They had camped many times along streams and rivers and had been successful in fishing and hunting small game and were able to save most of the dried buffalo jerky they had taken when leaving their village. They were trying to be wise about food reserves for a return trip, if they were not able to find buffalo on this hunt. No one of the Oglala Lakota Indians likes to be hungry and take unnecessary chances when given the choice to be prepared.

The three have been gone for twenty days and traveled many miles and were about to break into the Yellow Stone River country. They made camp by the fast-moving waters of a mountain stream and were talking by their campfire. Ciqala, is talking about their brother, Mato Ḣota (the grizzly bear) Titakuye (the immediate relatives), who brought many hogleglega (the grass pike, or the rainbow fish) for them to eat and some to take to their village.

The three are enjoying the sounds from the rapidly moving waters from the nearby mountain stream rushing over and around rocks. Life is good and it is good to be young and an Oglala Lakota brave, along with having a new grizzly bear brother as a new friend and all at the same time thinks Okiziwakiya, as he lay in his warm blanket later in the night.

Luzahan speaks up loudly, "I could eat two big rainbow trout by myself and carry one in each cheek after my belly is big and I can eat no more." Okiziwakiya laughing says, "Be happy to chew on dried tatanka jerky we have saved for this time and we do not go hungry." He continues in a more serious tone, "We will begin the hunt for fresh meat at sunrise. We must find a pteoptaye (buffalo herd) and take two only, for our horses to carry and pull a šun'onk'onpa (a pony or dog travois). We must

A Young Woman's Dance and A Brave Rescue

cut drag poles and smaller tree limbs to make our šun'onk'onpa, before we leave the trees and start across the land of grass, we may not find small trees there," Okiziwakiya tells his brothers.

The three young braves are moving slowly out of the trees in the morning with their extra horses each rigged with a šun'onk'onpa ready for a successful hunt. They are very alert to all around them. Okiziwakiya is first to see tracks of some tatanka moving southwest and speaks up, "Keep careful iyakita (to have an eye on, keep watch on) and follow these tracks, only a few tatanka, but that is enough, if we can get two, that is all we must take. Mother Earth will have given all we need as her gift to our hunt. Move our horses faster and let us find the tatanka before the sunsets in the sky and we lose their tracks to ahinhan (to rain upon, to fall as rain does on things)."

The three move out on their horses, at a steady trot, leading their three extra horses rigged with šun'onk'onpa in the direction of the mixed tatanka's hoof tracks, which they have left in the earth as a sign. This sign left in the dirt leads the three braves as a map written by nature's own hand.

The sun's light is fading and still no sign of any tatanka and Okiziwakiya is just about to call the end of day to make camp, when just over a small ridge ahead of them the noise of someone suffering was heard. The three braves halt and dismount. Ciqala holds the six horses and keeps them quiet, as Okiziwakiya and Luzahan move in slowly and quietly in their soft taha (deerskin) hanpa (moccasins) to see what is happening over the ridge in front of them. What they see after crawling to the ridge top, is a young brave from the Crow tribe, staked out with his hands and feet spread out tied to four stakes driven in the ground.

Four Indian braves from the Jicarilla Apache —one of

several bands of Apache Indians, currently living in New Mexico— tribe, ranging out from southwest on killing raids have taken a Crow wayaka (a captive taken in war, a prisoner) and have been torturing him with fire brands —sticks that have fire on one end.

Okiziwakiya whispers in Luzahan's left ear declaring, "Luzahan, we will save this young wayaka (a captive or prisoner of war). We are outnumbered but, we can charge in on our horses and try to scare them off. They have never seen horses. If they don't run, we will shoot our arrows at them from a distance on our horses and draw them away from their prisoner. Go tell Ciqala my plan and bring up all the horses, after he takes the šun'onk'onpa off the iwaglamnas (a spare or fresh horse) to a place halfway up the ridge, so we can mount them out of sight of the enemy Jicarilla Apache."

The three Oglala Lakota braves are about to fight in their first battle and are calling on all the bravery they have and say a prayer to Tatanka Ska Son for victory. Ciqala's duty is to lead the three extra horses behind his horse at a full run and Okiziwakiya and Luzahan will shoot arrows with their bows. If the enemy does not run, they may die, but they cannot watch this torture and do nothing. They are braves now and they must try to save the Crow brave from torture and certain death from the cruel acts of the Jicarilla Apache.

The three young Oglala Lakota braves with all their horses building up speed, burst over the small ridge with their horses at a full run, galloping and screaming at the top of their lungs the Oglala Lakota zuya (to go out with a war party, to make war, to lead out a war party) and šicahowawa (to cry out) the 'Oglala Lakota war cry'.

A Young Woman's Dance and A Brave Rescue

The four Jicarilla Apache raiding party are completely surprised and run away, but not before one let's go an arrow from his bow and his arrow hits Luzahan in the left shoulder, just below his collar bone. Luzahan drops his bow and reaches for his spear and throws it with his right hand, hitting the enemy brave high in his left leg going deep in his thigh. He falls and the others run away and leave him, like cowardly coyotes. This cowardly act is not a brotherly thing to do as a warrior, but fear rules them not bravery.

Okiziwakiya and Ciqala let the cowardly enemy go and gather around Luzahan, who has dismounted and is sitting down. Okiziwakiya shouts, "Ciqala, go stand guard over our wayaka, while I free his Crow wayaka and see what has happened to him, but first I will look at Luzahan," which he does. Ciqala passes by the Crow brave staked out on the ground and sees that he has an arrow in his lower right leg and one in his left hip and he also has some burns on his stomach, chest and arms from the torture by the cruel Jicarilla Apache warriors. He approaches the enemy Jicarilla Apache and guards him at the tip of his spear. Okiziwakiya is beside the wounded Luzahan and calls out to Ciqala, "Ciqala free the prisoner and bring him to me."

Ciqala feels he is very important as he warns the Jicarilla Apache prisoner to stay where he is in sign language. He goes to  free the Crow brave and helps him over to a place close to his brother Okiziwakiya, who is calling upon Wakantanka in a soft chanting way, and asking Him for the power of healing. Wakantanka speaks from far away, in a voice only heard by Okiziwakiya, 'Heal the enemy Jicarilla Apache first, give him some water and tatanka jerky, and tell him to go in peace, use napeonwoglaka (sign language), he will understand, as I will make it so. Heal the wounded Crow brave next and then you may heal Luzahan last'.

Okiziwakiya, as told by Wakantanka, quickly goes to the Jicarilla Apache warrior and lays his hands on both of his shoulders, looks him in the eyes and then with one hand pulls the spear from his leg. The Jicarilla Apache does not move or cry out in pain, for he has felt none and to his surprise, even the hole the spear thrown by Luzahan has made in his leg has disappeared. After standing up for a moment testing his leg in disbelief of it being healed, the newly healed Jicarilla Apache brave drops to his knees in a gesture of wapetokeca (a mark or sign, a miracle) an action performed to convey one's feelings or intentions of honoring, but Okiziwakiya stands him up on his feet, gives him some water and dried buffalo meat and motions him away. He turns and runs swiftly away on his healed left leg as if he had never been injured.

The Jicarilla Apache brave is heading in the direction which his cowardly companions have fled after leaving him behind, and they will most assuredly be surprised to see him again and to hear his story and maybe feel some scorn, for leaving him to the enemy's possible mistreatment and torture, which is their culture and way.

After Okiziwakiya pulls the arrows from the Crow brave, he heals his burns and gives him mni (water) from his walega (the bladder – walega miniyaye: a water jug) to drink. The wounded Crow brave is very grateful to be saved and amazed at what he has seen happen before his eyes.

Now it is Luzahan's turn to be healed as Wakantanka had directed Okiziwakiya to do. Okiziwakiya asked, "Are you in pain, my brother"? "No, my brother, my pain was stopped, when

A Young Woman's Dance and A Brave Rescue

you were chanting to Wakantanka," he answered. Luzahan continues, "I will ask you to remove this arrow stuck in me, even without pain, it looks bad and the maidens in our village will not look upon me with favor." Okiziwakiya and Ciqala laugh at Luzahan's words, but mostly the laugh is a laugh of relief felt after this battle has favored them.

Okiziwakiya removes the arrow from Luzahan's left shoulder and amazingly, Luzahan shows no pain as the enemy Jicarilla Apache arrow is pulled from his shoulder, along with its large flint arrowhead. All blood disappears beneath his shirt, as well as any sign of his wound. The hole in his taha shirt, remains as a badge of bravery shown in battle when he is seen by all his villagers upon his return from the hunt, and he is glad for that mark of battle to be seen by all, worn as a badge of courage, all thanks to Wakantanka, as He had planned this mark of bravery to be read by all the Oglala Lakota who see Luzahan and know his campfire story.

The Crow brave is completely amazed and is further awed by these unnatural acts of healing and mercy shown to him, which he has witnessed with his own eyes this day. Later at the end of the day, he is given some food as he sits around the campfire wrapped in a woven šunkawakan (horse) hair blanket given him for warmth around the campfire and for sleeping on the ground among his new friends the Oglala Lakota braves. His new friends, who saved him and healed him of his terrible wounds, he knows he would have surely died a pain filled death, if they had not chosen to risk their lives to save him. He must help them or serve them in any way if it is in his power to do so. He would do this gladly, in order to repay their kindness and the bravery shown, in order to save one who is not from their tribe, from the evil fearsome Jicarilla Apache raiders.

He has never known the Oglala Lakota to be so kind and strong, as he has never been in contact with any Oglala Lakota before this day. The healer one, Okiziwakiya, is surely blessed by the Creator, because no other, could perform such a wakanyan (in a sacred manner, in a holy, or wonderful or even a mysterious way) an act or miracle. What he does not understand is why Okiziwakiya, healed the enemy Jicarilla Apache and him before his own brother Luzahan, who he healed last of all.

The Crow brave will soon know the answer, that Wakantanka has shown him mercy and kindness because Okiziwakiya is showing him that, even as an enemy and stranger. This man has great value and love to share, through the Will of Wakantanka, who is using Okiziwakiya, as His example of love and kindness to be shown all captured enemies and strangers, for they will tell their own campfire story about how they were treated. We are all Wakantanka's children and He loves us all. We must treat our brothers kindly for that is our duty on Mother Earth, according to His will.

The early morning sun brings the camp to life as a campfire is lit by Luzahan and the four braves gather around it, seated with their blankets around their shoulders, warming themselves while eating dried meat and berries. Through sign language, the Crow brave tells his new friends his name's meaning, he is Arikara 'A-rik-a-ra' (running wolf - Crow dialect).

The three motion in sign language, that they are hunting tatanka. Arikara motions in signing, for the Oglala Lakota braves to follow him and starts to walk away, but Okiziwakiya stops him and points to one of his iwaglamnas (an extra or fresh horse) and helps him up on its back. Arikara is to ride on him for now, although Okiziwakiya has other plans about this act of consideration for another time.

A Young Woman's Dance and A Brave Rescue

Arikara is being led behind Okiziwakiya and yells out in his Crow dialect, "Go there" which, even though the Oglala Lakota braves do not understand, his sign language motion with his hand pointing, directs them in a south westerly direction. Soon after traveling just short of a mile in distance, they spot a small group of tatanka grazing in a low area some distance out from them. Okiziwakiya speaks, "Ciqala, stay with the iwaglamnas and have our new friend Arikara hold two to help you keep them calm. Luzahan and I will hunt from horses." Ciqala answers, "As you speak it, brother." Ciqala has great respect for his brother Okiziwakiya and does not complain or raise objections to his will. Okiziwakiya motions Arikara to stay with Ciqala and he and Luzahan will charge at the tatankas at full gallop on their fast horses.

Okiziwakiya closes in on the first big bull tatanka with his faithful šunkawakan, and brings it down with his spear. Luzahan shoots another with his bow and a hunting arrow and hits it in the neck, but the big bull does not go down and it turns, charging at Luzahan. Luzahan's horse makes a quick side-stepping move and the big bull tatanka's horn on the side of his head just misses Luzahan's šunkawakan rear leg. Circling around, Luzahan has to chase the wounded bull tatanka down and finish its life from suffering with his well thrown spear reaching straight to the heart of the bull tatanka and he falls dead, skidding to a halt on his left side.

The four braves work hard field dressing (cleaning and processing) the two big tatanka's fresh meat and haul it wrapped in their own buffalo hides, back to the tree line, where they must build fires and make racks out of tree limbs and smoke the meat cut in thin strips, as they have been taught by their mothers, who will be most grateful they were not a part of this hard work. It is too far a journey back to the Oglala Lakota village, to take the fresh killed meat and the job to clean and smoke the tatanka meat must be done now to save it from becoming kuka (rotten).

This smoking of the two big tatanka's meat takes many days to complete, but the four young braves work hard and surprisingly, Arikara works the hardest of all. He has been a big help to his new friends and seems very loyal to them.

During this smoking of meat time, Okiziwakiya has been teaching Arikara how to ride and care for horses. He learns quickly and Okiziwakiya is pleased with his attitude and willingness to help his new Oglala Lakota friends. Arikara is winning all three Oglala Lakota braves respect and trust, by his willingness to work hard and his knowledge of cleaning and smoking the tatanka meat, not to mention his knowledge of hunting and finding tatanka. He also helps with night guard duty and is trusted by his new friends, brother braves.

When the dried and smoked tatanka meat has been loaded on the tušuheyunpi (the travois) behind two of the extra horses, Okiziwakiya loads the little remaining meat on his horse behind him. Then he hands the reins of the horse he has been leading beside him with Arikara riding happily aboard up until now. Okiziwakiya now gifts Arikara this horse, as a gift to ride for years to come and return with this great honor to his tribe. Arikara is over joyed and can't thank Okiziwakiya, Luzahan and Ciqala, enough for saving his life and all the kindness they have shone to him. He becomes solemn as he turns from his new brothers and departs, riding toward his village far away. He is much too sad to look back at his new friends, as he rides away on his prized šunkawakan.

Soon however his thoughts turn to excitement, as he thinks about returning to his Crow village people with this great gift and an incredible campfire story that will carry down through the ages among his tribe members, as all tribal history is passed forward to the young. His new horse they have never seen will help them believe his story. Life is good now that he knows and believes in Wakantanka and His Son, Tatanka Ska Son, and he will believe in Them always and tell what he has learned about Them to all his tribe around many campfires.

Until we share our next Campfire Story Telling - "Man of the Sun," Tatanka Ska Son wants you to spread the words of this campfire story to all who will listen. May Wakantanka be with you.

Oglala Lakota brave offering up love and praise to Wakantanka in prayer

Heȟaka

Chapter 8

Man of the Sun

An early morning sunrise finds Okiziwakiya (cause to heal up), Luzahan (swift) and Ciqala (little one) with their spare horses pulling travois loaded with smoked tatanka (buffalo) meat, heading back to their village, where many have been worried, —most especially the mothers of the three long overdue braves— about their long absence. Not Chief Matoskah (white bear), Okiziwakiya's father, who believes his son, is watched over by Tatanka Ska Son.

Chief Matoskah believes his son will return safe, no

doubt with many stories to be told by many campfires upon his return to the village and he looks forward to hearing them all in detail. The chief gives these words to his wife, Winona (first born daughter), to calm her concerns about her son, but still she worries as do most loving mothers, whom the Creator has made to be so, to protect His children. Even among the animals many will fight to the death to protect their young.

Women are the heart of the Oglala (to scatter one's own) band and the Lakota (The Siouan people) Nation and bare the children, teach children, and braves of the tribe in the proper ways of the Wakantanka (The Great Spirit, the Creator, God). Love and mercy are the treasure they carry in their hearts and they bear the troubles of the village upon their backs. The women are revered among the Oglala Lakota people and are highly respected and any man who abuses a female is shunned by all. The Oglala Lakota customs are an honorable way to live among Mother Earth and respect for her gifts of nature and home, all based on honoring the care given to her each day.

When the three braves arrive in their village there is great joy and pride among the people for these young braves have been gone for many wihiyalas (the passing of the sun) and now are returning with much bounty in food for the villagers. Okiziwakiya is pleased when Wachiwi (dancing girl) comes to honor him and when she does, he hands her some of the tatanka smoked meat, which she very thankfully accepts as a gift for her and her family. She has missed him yutkeya (deeply, as said of a bluff shore where the water is deep) and held him in her heart in a special place where only he can live and be nourished and has worried about his well-being while he has been away. She now knows for sure, no other brave can ever find this special place in her heart or be so loved by her, as is Okiziwakiya on this special day.

Man of the Sun

Meanwhile, Arikara (running wolf – Crow dialect) is on his way heading back to his village, and is riding his new hinto (gray horse) horse (iichiile – a horse – Crow dialect) given to him by Okiziwakiya, and thinking of how lucky he has been to be saved from his mortal enemy and the mortal enemy of his Crow (Apsáalooke – children of the large-beaked bird – Siouan language) Indian tribe, the Jicarilla Apache —one of several bands of Apache Indians, currently living in New Mexico. He is keeping a watchful eye out for any sign of this enemy. He knows he can now easily outrun any who would come against him, if he can see them first on Hinto, his horse's new name.

Arikara is making camp near a stream with good visibility in all directions and he has hobbled —to tie a leather strap around both front legs, just above the fetlocks on the cannon bone. A fetlock is the lower leg joint nearest to the pastern —an area between the fetlock and the top of the hoof— of Hinto, who is grazing —feeding on grass— nearby in a grassy area, so she could easily feed quietly close by Arikara's campsite, when all of a sudden, a bright blue colored light tube comes down by his campfire.

Arikara stands motionless as Tatanka Ska Son appears before him. Arikara the Crow brave, is fearful and remembers that he has seen Tatanka Ska Son long ago, when He was flying over his head with three young Indians on His Sacred Back. Tatanka Ska Son says, "Fear not, for I am Tatanka Ska Son, a Brother of your three friends Okiziwakiya, Luzahan and Ciqala, who saved you with a little help from Me and through their own bravery. You saw Us flying over you many moons ago, and you only told your mother of this story, and she advised you to keep the story to yourself. I have another secret you must never tell anyone about, even your mother."

Arikara asks, "I kneel to You in thanks and ask what I may do to please and serve You"? Tatanka Ska Son states, "I say to you, you must believe in Me and believe that I, Tatanka Ska Son, Am the true Son of Wakantanka, The Great Spirit, the Creator, God, and that is all I ask of you now."

Tatanka Ska Son continues speaking to Arikara, "If you will be faithful to My Father's Wishes, and trust in Him always, you will be blessed with great strength far beyond that of many strong braves put together as a force against you. You, Arikara, will free your people of the evil Jicarilla Apache and their evil thoughts and actions against them. You will be able to defeat them by your own hand. Any other Indian tribes and any possible harm they have put upon your tribe in the past, are not to be punished.

"All vengeance is Mine and only I will judge wrong doing. I will send you to destroy any who war against you or your tribe, with great strength in battle and be beside you always.

"You will become chief of your Crow tribe very soon, and lead them for many years. Hear My Words closely, your great strength, will be with you as long as you have your hinto and keep her in good health, she will serve you well. When she is gone from your care, through some negligence by you, you will lose your great strength, unless your Father, Wakantanka, thinks you worthy of His trust to rule your tribe and then your strength will be at hand.

"Tell no one of this My Words of the secret of your strength, or you will surely lose all that I have given you this day. You will only tell stories of Me and My Father, the Creator

Wakantanka and My visit to you, but not of the secret of the hinto, which I have asked you to keep secretly in your heart."

Tatanka Ska Son lifts off and returns into the sky, leaving Arikara alone, and very soon, great strength begins to flow through him, like a swift mountain stream flows through the earth and he can feel it's tingling of warmth, as Mother Earth surely must feel, filled with all of nature's wonders running through her veins.

Arikara reaches his village and as he enters, all the villagers gather and stare at the sight of Arikara riding on an animal they have never seen and are amazed as he rides Hinto through the village. He sees that some of the tipis (teepee or tent or lodge) have been burned and many women are wailing in pain at the loss of husbands and sons. Their village was attacked by the Jicarilla Apache and many prisoners' mostly young Crow girls were taken.

When Arikara reaches his mother's unburned tipi, made of twenty five ptehašla (buffalo hide without the hair) he finds out from other villagers, that his father Cheéte (che-é-te - wolf – in Crow dialect) has been killed and his mother Swan (bii-lee - in Crow dialect) and sister Fish (bua – in Crow dialect) have been taken by the enemy Jicarilla Apache ten days past.

Arikara honors his father's death with a dance and song of sorrow, repeated many times, then he asks some braves to come with him to rescue his mother and sister, but he can find no one willing to go, except for one, Turtle (bas-axe – in Crow dialect). Turtle, a boy of only eleven seasons, but known to his villagers to be brave and is big for his age. Turtle is wise for his years, because he has listened closely among the tribal elder's council fires, while others his age played Crow games with each other.

His mother, has taught him well in the ways of life and about Mother Earth, who is to be forever respected and honored, by Turtle throughout his life.

Arikara pulls Turtle up behind him on Hinto, his gray horse, at sunrise and leaves his village. Turtle, is to ride behind him on this rescue mission. He is thrilled to be taken along on this great rescue mission and riding on Hinto is truly an honor.

One mighty Crow brave and one Crow boy head off in the direction of the enemy Jicarilla Apache raiding warriors. Arikara is hoping to find all the Crow captives alive. After five days travel, dangerous eyes are watching them as they crisscross through many large boulders and tall trees. Three large igmuwatoglas (mountain lion) await them nearby. A big mother mountain lion has spotted the two Crow braves riding on a hinto and plans to make this her last opportunity of teaching hunting skills to her two young male cubs. Her two cubs are almost as big as she is and nearly ready to go out on their own.

They await their mother's hunting lesson on how to take down this strange beast with three heads, none of which have they ever seen before. The three mountain lions are in a crouching position waiting for the Crow brave and his young companion Turtle on a hinto, to come into range for them to strike.

Hinto senses danger, but does not stop and continues moving forward urged on by Arikara's gentle riding skills. The three mountain lions launch their sprint and leap in on the attack, pouncing on the three headed prey they have been stalking. Both Arikara and Turtle are knocked off Hinto and each young Crow is attacked separately by the young mountain lion brothers, while mother mountain lion jumps on Hinto's back, which puts the gray horse into full flight, at a dead running gallop, trying to shake the mother mountain lion off her back.

There is no time to use their weapons, so Arikara jumps to his feet and tears the mountain lion off his back and slings it far away into the sunlight. He then grabs the second young mountain lion off of Turtle, who is rolling on the ground holding the mountain lion's mouth away from his face by its cheeks. Arikara slings him in the same direction he threw his brother mountain lion. The second mountain lion hits his brother mountain lion very hard and they lay together, whimpering and injured, but alive. Both having learned a hard lesson this day, they will never attack a three headed animal again. Arikara sees his hinto has bolted with mother mountain lion on her back and is running hard trying to shake off this enemy.

Mother mountain lion has locked herself on with claws and paws and is biting Hinto on the neck. Arikara's hinto is scared and desperate to get the mountain lion off her back, so she begins to buck, crow hopping (jumping into the air using all four feet at one time) and kicking out with her back hooves, all to no avail. Still not giving-in to the mother mountain lion's vicious attack, Hinto remains on her feet.

Arikara has been running after his terrified hinto. He is completely surprised at how fast he can run now, with his gift of new strength from Wakantanka. Arikara is running faster than any deer or elk he has ever seen and quickly catches up to his hinto, jumps up on her back, landing behind the mountain lion, and pulls the hungry mountain lion's jaws open and off his horse's neck. He does this easily with his new mighty bare hands, gripping her head and pulling her jaws apart, releasing her strong bite on his gray horse's neck, like pulling a fish from the water. Arikara then throws the female mountain lion back into the trees, like a baby bird without the strength to fly. His mighty hands are unscathed, being blessed with great strength and protection by Wakantanka, the Creator and Tatanka Ska Son, His Son.

Mother mountain lion lands in a heap, stunned for a moment by her hard landing. She gets-up, shakes, freeing her slick golden colored fur from leaves and dirt. She realizes she has made a mistake in taking on this strange animal, who can divide itself and then fight to help its other parts to defeat her so easily. She slowly heads in the direction of her two young mountain lion sons, hoping they are unhurt.

Mother mountain lion and young sons, have truly met their

match today when they ran into the mighty Arikara and Turtle of the Crow tribe and Hinto, a strange animal she has never seen before. One thought in her head is, she will never attack any "three headed animals," no never ever again. She counts herself to be lucky to live, along with her sons.

This attack by the three mountain lions is Arikara's first real test of his new strength, —which he was promised by Wakantanka— and he knows Wakantanka has truly blessed him with this great strength and he is ready to face all enemies with his new strength and power, but most of all by his complete trust in Wakantanka.

Turtle cannot believe what he has seen. Later by their late-night campfire, Arikara tells him the story of his encounter with the Oglala Lakota braves and his meeting with Tatanka Ska Son and this truly sacred story he has lived to tell about. Turtle is a new believer after hearing Arikara's stories and he has decided he will follow Arikara forever in this life, as a faithful brother believer and will become a great 'Story Teller' in the many moons to come, and he will be respected among many in his Crow tribe for his campfire story telling abilities.

The two Crow make camp by a stream and Arikara washes the wounds on his hinto and rubs them with dried healing leaves he has carried with him to treat injuries, in his mission to save his mother and sister and any of the other Crow hostages held by the evil Jicarilla Apache raiders. He also treats some cuts and scratches on Turtle, from his fight with the young mountain lion that attacked him. Arikara's hinto is healing well, but has been too injured to carry the two the next day, with deep scratches on his back. Not wanting to lose the trail of the Jicarilla Apache on foot, Arikara and Turtle leave at the early dawn's light, taking turns leading Arikara's faithful gray horse Hinto. They travel all day and into the night, until they are stopped by total darkness.

They will "cold camp" —no campfire use— from now on, as

they close in on their enemy, not wanting to be discovered by the Jicarilla Apache, in case they are close enough to have a campfire spotted by a rear guard or scout, which the evil ones may have posted at night. Arikara believes they will soon catch up with the Jicarilla Apache raiders, from the signs he is reading, from following their trail and reading their campfires for signs of use.

Arikara's gray horse has healed well enough to ride again and the next six day's travel brings them within one half mile of the Jicarilla Apache, who are camped by a river and have built a large campfire and a few small ones, made by out of camp night guards. These campfires can be seen by Arikara and Turtle from their cold camp, on a hill above the river directly in front of them in the distance.

Arikara speaks, "Turtle, we will ride in on Hinto at full speed and attack the Jicarilla Apache while most are sleeping. How many Jicarilla Apache did you see"? Turtle answers, "I saw at least thirty or forty, before I was knocked out by a blow to my head, by a big Jicarilla Apache brave's fist at our Crow village. I am glad he did not use a club or I could not tell this story again." Arikara says, "I am also glad, my little brother, I will need you to help me, I have a plan. I will go and scout the camp and you stay with my hinto until I return." Turtle nods and says, "As you say, mighty one."

Arikara is walking at a fast pace and then runs a fast few hundred feet across a clearing in the moonlight, like an antelope and disappears into the trees close to the enemy camp. Arikara starts his slow crawl to within two hundred feet of the Jicarilla Apache camp.

The Jicarilla Apache camp fires have died down, but Arikara

has already seen his mother and sister, along with about twenty other women and young girls, bound and staked to the ground, by dying campfires. They are being guarded by three Jicarilla Apache braves.

After scouting more around the Jicarilla Apache camp, Arikara sees there are only two other braves on guard on the outskirts of the main camp. One of the night guards is near the river and the other guard is within one hundred feet of the direction he plans to attack from. Arikara decides to relieve the guard on duty between the two camps, before he and Turtle attack on horseback. He decides to do this, so he and Turtle can gain more of a surprise when they attack the main camp.

Arikara moves in very quietly and hits the brave with his fist, knocking him out and grabs the big Jicarilla Apache brave by the neck with his left hand and clamps his right hand over his mouth and lifts him up before his limp body hits the ground and makes any noise. He carries him away from the camp over his mighty right shoulder and then he runs fast across the open clearing, carrying his prisoner back toward his cold camp and Turtle, never slowing his pace, even though his prisoner's weight would slow any other person carrying him to a slow walk. Now the Jicarilla Apache brave wakes up on the way back to where Turtle is waiting. Arikara again knocks him unconscious to keep him quiet.

The two Crow braves bind and gag the Jicarilla Apache brave to a tree with deer skin twine, while he is still out cold, but he wakes up and starts to squirm and tries to make noises, moaning and struggling. Arikara walks up to him, looks him in the eyes and shakes his head in a way of napeonwoglaka (using sign language with hand motions and gestures) to communicate a message to him, that message was, that he must remain calm and quiet or he will be killed immediately. Arikara gives him a strong squeeze on his arm and the Jicarilla Apache brave understands Arikara's meaning by the strength in his grip, which nearly crushes his arm, and he becomes very quiet and subdued in his actions. He is amazed to see the two Crow ride off on a strange beast, the likes of which he has never seen. He is terrified, but remains quiet, as he has been duly warned.

Arikara and Turtle dismount about five hundred feet from the Jicarilla Apache camp. It is good for them that the swift running river has blocked out the silence of the night with her sweet song, giving them cover from any noise they might make and Hinto's movements. The two slowly walk within one hundred yards of the Jicarilla Apache camp, mount up on Hinto and go forward at a walk and then run at a gallop —the gallop is the fastest gait or running pace, that can be performed by a horse— as fast as they can dodge between the trees through the semi-darkness of the late moon's light.

The plan unfolding, is for Arikara to take out the three Jicarilla Apaches guarding his mother, sister and other women and girls, leaving Turtle to protect them from any other Jicarilla Apache that may be left, if they get by Arikara or if he is overcome by their numbers.

It is a good plan made by Arikara. The Jicarilla Apache camp is completely caught off guard not expecting any attack from any other raiding warriors. Arikara guides Hinto into where the three outer camp guards that have his mother and the others staked out. He quickly dismounts, leaving Turtle on foot holding on to Hinto by his bridle and then he instantly grabs the first Jicarilla Apache brave, swings his body around one time and hits the other two guards, who have rushed him, killing all three. All this happened so fast, the three Jicarilla Apache could not fight him with their knives.

Arikara, runs swiftly throughout the Jicarilla Apache camp, using his stone headed wicat'e (an instrument with which to kill) and destroys the entire encampment of forty-four braves, as they charge him in groups of four or five. All this ferocious fighting lasting only a matter of two minutes, in hand to hand combat.

Some Jicarilla Apache warriors tried to shoot arrows into Arikara, but he used the body of one of the warriors he killed as a shield and charged them using his stone headed tomahawk in his attack upon them. Arikara tossed the dead Jicarilla Apache he has used as a shield, at remaining Jicarilla Apache braves, knocking them to the ground to receive his heavy stone headed tomahawk blows and end their evil ways. He only suffers small wounds to each powerful arm, after this his first great battle against many wimacas (men).

The Jicarilla Apache guard by the river has heard the commotion of the fighting in camp and runs in sight of the camp and sees Arikara in action, destroying all his Jicarilla Apache brothers like an owamniomni (a cyclone) among a field of corn. He sees this one-sided battle by one super human Crow warrior. He becomes terrified and turns, sprinting away at a full run toward the river. The Jicarilla Apache guard crosses the river falling twice before reaching the other side of the river and heads off at a full run toward his village two days away by foot into the west. He looks back and no one is following him, so he slows down to a steady run, putting as much distance as he can muster, away from the most powerful warrior he has ever seen.

He is thinking and hoping his villagers believe the story he has to tell them, when he arrives empty handed, with no other warriors in his raiding party by his side to verify his story. They may think he is a deserter, along with being a liar.

Arikara goes to his mother and sister and frees them, while Turtle frees the other Crow women, maidens and young girls. There is much hugging among the captives and joy shared by the two, who have saved them from the Jicarilla Apache warriors and certain slavery and an early death, once they could not serve as directed by their captors. Swan, Arikara's mother says, "My son, how strong you are, as no other, tell Swan story"? Arikara tells Swan, "Wakantanka, as the Oglala Lakota call Him, the Creator, God, has sent His Son they call, Tatanka Ska Son, in the form of a white buffalo (Bi'Shee – Crow dialect). It is He who gave me this great strength in my hands, arms and legs. A great strength to serve our people and save all from our enemies, who may come against us. Let us go from this place of killing, and be far away from this place of sadness by tomorrow's moon."

Arikara's sister, Fish, gives her brother a big hug and says, "My brother, you have saved us, we were mistreated by the Jicarilla Apache braves and slaves to them. You, Arikara, are to be honored forever by our people and me, your sister, Fish, honors you now." Arikara replies, "All thanks to Wakantanka, the Creator, who gives me great strength in my arms and the speed of a swift wolf in my legs." Fish replies, "As you say my brother, before my eyes, as I have seen, it is so."

The young maidens, women and young girls are led by Arikara, who has Swan and Fish riding upon the back of Hinto and the rest of the women and girls are on foot, following closely behind. Some distance further behind them, young Turtle has rear guard responsibilities, walking proudly after this battle hoping he will be honored by the tribal elders as a brave, upon returning to their village when they hear the stories of Arikara's rescue mission and the part he played. Although, he did not have to fight, he did not fail to do as he was told by Arikara and was ready to give his life to protect the Crow captives. This did not go unnoticed by Arikara or the others who were freed from the Jicarilla Apache enemy. Turtle is on his way to becoming a brave among his tribe very soon, because Arikara will make it so.

When Arikara returns with Turtle and all Crow captives, he will be given a new name, as is most fitting, considering his bravery. He will be named by his village chief and be called wimaca (a man) of wiyohiyanpa (the east sun rising), "Man of the rising sun – in the English language" and he will be known to many very soon, by his very shortened Crow new name Sun (axxaashe – Crow dialect) Man (bachhee – Crow dialect). "Sun Man – in the English language."

Until our next adventure Campfire Story Telling - "Sun Man's Rescue Sends a Strong Message," may you walk a straight path with all trust in Wakantanka to guide you. He will Bless and watch over you by your campfires in all of life's travels. His love is eternal.

Young Lakota girl at her family tipi

*Oglala Lakota going on
the trail of tatanka*

Chapter 9

Sun Man's Rescue Sends a Strong Message

Okiziwakiya (to cause to heal up) has shared his story of the great buffalo hunt with all the villagers and they have listened to every word with great interest and many have expressed in words, they believe in Wakantanka and His Son, Tatanka Ska Son. Okiziwakiya's father, Chief Matoskah (white bear), has been wrestling with a bad feeling about the far-ranging Jicarilla Apache —one of several bands of Apache Indians, currently living in New Mexico— raiders and of their possible success in finding his village to attack and spoil. He has posted extra guards further out from the village for addition security.

He tells Okiziwakiya, his son, to wait for iomaka (the next year) and then he is to go to visit his new Crow (Apsáalooke – children of the large-beaked bird – Siouan language) brother Arikara (Running Wolf – Crow dialect) and learn if the Jicarilla Apaches have come back to his village for revenge. Also, if he thinks they may come this far to attack the Oglala (to scatter one's own) Lakota (the Siouan people) village to get women as slaves and steal horses, as they may have seen the horses he had, before he released the Jicarilla Apache raider, he healed from Luzahan's (swift) spear wound. This all happened before he healed and gave a horse to Arikara, his Crow brave friend.

Okiziwakiya is unaware of knowing about Arikara's great trouble with the Jicarilla Apache raid on Arikara's village. The Jicarilla Apache most certainly have learned from the Jicarilla Apache brave, who escaped Arikara when he killed all their raiders and rescued his family and other Crow captives. Okiziwakiya is without this knowledge and is working on his plan, to take a burden of worry from his father's mind. Okiziwakiya agrees that his father's plan is good with much wisdom and forward thinking and he would follow his plan. His father is a wise chief and not just his father, but as chief he is father of the entire village and he is also responsible for their safety.

Okiziwakiya has another idea that he believes will erase this

Sun Man's Rescue Sends a Strong Message

worry and burden carried by his father, which his father carries very heavily in his heart. Okiziwakiya plans to go sooner on this mission, than his father has requested and begins by recruiting his brothers Luzahan and Ciqala (little one).

The two Oglala Lakota brothers agree with great appreciation to serve on Okiziwakiya's special mission and they keep these plans to themselves. The three slip away after many days of planning, on a dark night after careful preparations, gathering supplies secretly for their impending travel, before the village is awake and active with morning chores by the women and young maidens with many eyes of the eagle and ears of the itunpsicala (the field mouse) in a silent winters' snowfall.

Having traveled a short distance from their village they are joined by Mato Hota (a grizzly bear) Titakuye (the immediate relatives), their new bear otakuye (brotherhood, relationship, relations, kinfolk, kinship) brother. Okiziwakiya has enlisted his mighty brown mato hota brother, to help him in his mission and he is not alone in forming a small army traveling to meet with Arikara and the Crow people.

Soon, they are joined by others while traveling through the deep forest. Okiziwakiya climbs down off his hinto (a gray horse) and lets out a loud long howling sound and all with him watch with great interest wondering what the reason is making Okiziwakiya howl out so loudly. Suddenly, coming in from all directions among the tall trees, a huge šungmanitu (a wolf) pack charges in to greet him, to the surprise of all except Okiziwakiya. He has called in his brother Šungmanitu (a wolf) Aitancan (the ruler over), Šungmanitu Aitancan (wolf ruler), to come to him and when he reaches Okiziwakiya's side he sits down, panting beside his Oglala Lakota friend.

His entire pack of twenty šungmanitus, sit down behind him and begin watching their leader's actions for signals to react to, or relax. Okiziwakiya rubs Šungmanitu Aitancan on his head. He reacts and licks his Oglala Lakota brave's hand in friendship, as a sign of affection and loving devotion.

Now Okiziwakiya has the army he feels he needs for the first part of his mission, which is to go to the Crow village, home of Arikara. Little does Okiziwakiya know of the great strength his Crow brother Arikara has been given by Wakantanka through His Son, Tatanka Ska Son.

The new army consisting of Oglala Lakota Indian braves, a big brown grizzly bear brother and a pack of friendly wolves are camped by a mountain stream, have just finished a meal of hogleglega (the grass pike or possibly a rainbow fish) cooked over campfire. Mato Hota Titakuye and Šungmanitu Aitancan and his brother šungmanitus are sharing a big elk, which big brown mato hota titakuye, has hunted down and brought into camp to share with his šungmanitu brothers.

This is the first of many campfire gatherings; this most unusual army will share. Also, a most important time when they bond as brothers on a common mission, all in the lap of Mother Earth and all she provides so freely, only asking for respect of her gifts and that they are not to be wasted or abused.

Okiziwakiya's army, one never before seen by human beings, is very near to the Crow village of Arikara. They have made camp and are enjoying a campfire meal when Okiziwakiya motions for Luzahan and Ciqala to come closer. He tells them that he plans on entering the Crow village alone the next day and for them to come into the Crow village in the late afternoon with Mato Ḣota Titakuye and Šungmanitu Aitancan and his pack of šungmanitu brothers. Okiziwakiya explains, this will give him time to prepare Arikara and his people for the presence of his unbelievable warriors, soon to visit their village.

An early morning raising sun finds Okiziwakiya approaching a young Crow brave on guard for his village. He approaches him very slowly after being challenged by this very alert Crow guard. He shows his hands held open with his palms facing toward the Crow brave, indicating he holds no weapons to be used in a planned attack, in a sign he clearly comes in peace. The guard alerts the villagers and Okiziwakiya, is immediately surrounded by Crow warriors. Okiziwakiya speaks, "Arikara! Take me to Arikara."

The Crow warriors move Okiziwakiya toward the tipi (teepee

or tent or lodge) of Wimaca (man – Lakota dialect) Wiyohiyanpa (the rising sun – in the Lakota dialect) Man of the Rising Sun, who has now come out in response to the voices he has heard. Seeing his brother Okiziwakiya, he gives out a great shout of joy, "Okiziwakiya, Okiziwakiya my brother in Wakantanka." Wiyohiyanpa Wimaca runs to greet Okiziwakiya and the two hug each other, in a welcome sign of affection and admiration for one another. All the Crow villagers see this and become friendly and all smile whenever Okiziwakiya looks at their faces.

Wiyohiyanpa Wimaca calls all the villagers together and a great celebration begins. Many campfires are started and Crow women begin cooking. Wiyohiyanpa Wimaca directs Okiziwakiya to his tipi. Wiyohiyanpa Wimaca in sign language explains first his new name Sun (axxaashe – Crow dialect), which is easily done in sign language and Man (bachhee – Crow dialect), however it is harder for 'Sun Man' to explain to Okiziwakiya his visit from Tatanka Ska Son and the great gift of strength Wakantanka has given him. So Axxaashe Bachhee tells Okiziwakiya of Tatanka Ska Son's visit in sign language and then he tries to explain about his gift of great strength from Wakantanka which Okiziwakiya does not understand.

That being so, 'Man of the Sun' (Axxaashe Bachhee), guides Okiziwakiya outside his tipi and takes him to a big boulder near his village. He points up to the sky, then with both hands he grabs the giant boulder, then lifts it up over his head and throws the big boulder over fifty feet away, with very little effort.

Okiziwakiya is amazed by this gift of great strengthen given by Wakantanka to his Crow friend Axxaashe Bachhee, but understands, that Wakantanka gives special gifts to those He loves and that trust in Him, for His purposes to be done upon Mother Earth. Okiziwakiya learns of his brother, 'Sun Man' —

Sun Man's Rescue Sends a Strong Message

which is the name we will use from now on in this story telling— and his mission to rescue his mother, sister and other captive Crow maidens from the enemy Jicarilla Apache raiders. He also learns that one escaped and may have returned to his village and warned of a Crow warrior who killed all but one, himself.

It would be doubtful that anyone would believe this story, and many did not, until no other Jicarilla Apaches who Sun Man has had battle with returned to their village. The Jicarilla Apache warriors decided to believe their Jicarilla Apache brother's story with some doubt, but planned to return in great numbers and avenge this defeat by the great and powerful Crow warrior, if he in fact exists, and take some more captive maidens as slaves. This raid would be a show of their strength as great warriors and they could avenge the loss of many of their Jicarilla Apache braves. It is to be zuya (war – Lakota dialect), never mind the story told.

Okiziwakiya is now more than ever worried about the possibility of avenging Jicarilla Apaches coming against Sun Man and his Crow people and against the Oglala Lakota people next. Okiziwakiya signs this meaning to Sun Man, who signs back asking, if Okiziwakiya believes the Jicarilla Apache will come again? Okiziwakiya nods his head in a 'yes' answer. Especially after learning the story of the battle and rescue of his family and others held prisoners by the enemy Jicarilla Apache, which his mighty Crow brother defeated. He explains in sign that he has a plan, a way to takpe (to come upon, attack) on the Jicarilla Apache raiders and makes a lasting peace treaty among the three tribes.

Sun Man signs again that he will listen to Okiziwakiya's council and tell his people at his campfire tonight. Okiziwakiya uses sign language to tell his plans, and that he has others that are coming and describes again in sign, the best he could, that some are great animal friends and for him and others of his village to not fear them, but welcome them into their village. He further tries to explain in sign language to the best of his ability 'signing, my brother, I have brought a small force of my brothers and those which your people will fear, until they know they come as titakuye (the immediate relatives), even you will wonder'. Okiziwakiya is not sure Sun Man understands, but knows he comes in friendship, and that will have to make it so for now.

Okiziwakiya leaves the Crow village and goes out to meet Luzahan, Ciqala, Mato Ḣota Titakuye, Šunkmanitu Aitancan (wolf ruler) and his pack of šungmanitu brothers. He must do so because he believes his presence with this strange, never before seen band of brothers, will help in keeping the Crow villagers from fearing, and attacking.

It will be an amazing sight to see when this small group of nature's mighty warriors of another blood, who come together for war against the enemy of the Oglala Lakota and Crow people, which dwell in these beautiful lands, enter the Crow village.

It is a good plan made by Okiziwakiya and Sun Man agrees to use it. This coming great zuya against an evil enemy is common to both of their tribes. Little do they know that a large group of over two hundred Jicarilla Apache warriors are heading toward the Crow village at this very moment and are closing in rapidly on foot.

Sun Man has been scouting for some time in the past few moons, after his battle with the Jicarilla Apache, in the direction of the Jicarilla Apache village location further south. He has found a narrow cliff ledge that passes through large borders on

Sun Man's Rescue Sends a Strong Message

both sides of a narrow cliff ledge. It is just beyond where he rescued his mother, sister and others some months before, when his name was Arikara (Running Wolf – Crow dialect).

Sun Man signs Okiziwakiya telling about this area of great defensive value, that the Jicarilla Apache must come through to reach the Crow village. They must get through to this area before any of the enemy might scout them and learn of their plan to attack them first. They must leave soon and begin the mission of attack against the Jicarilla Apache.

Okiziwakiya reaches Luzahan, Ciqala and his brothers of the woods. All are glad to see him and gather around him in a warm welcome. Okiziwakiya, "My brothers, follow me into the Crow village by twos. I will lead, Luzahan, you and Ciqala will walk side by side, behind me, our mighty Mato Hota Titakuye and Šungmanitu Aitancan will walk side by side and all šungmanitu pack warriors will walk behind Šungmanitu Aitancan two by two. It will make a good showing of Mother Earth's creatures and all will be welcome." Okiziwakiya's band of warriors head out of their camp to the Crow village and reach the edge of the village an hour before sunset.

All the Crow villagers are standing in total silence. They are completely struck with amazement; they can hardly believe their eyes at the sight of a great brown grizzly bear and big gray wolves tamely, following the three Oglala Lakota braves into their village.

They are relieved when Sun Man, welcomes them and puts all his Crow villagers at ease. Sun Man calls for a big campfire to be made in the middle of the Crow village and for all Crow to gather to hear his words. He tells them that he fears the Jicarilla Apache are planning an attack on them and that he, along with

Okiziwakiya, Luzahan, Ciqala and his special army of wild animal warrior brothers will go out to find the Jicarilla Apache village and meet the enemy in battle.

They will leave in two days at sun's first light. Two days of preparing for war will have to be all the time they can spare before leaving the Crow village. For tonight they will eat, dance and sing songs, honoring Wakantanka and His new warriors sent to help them.

Two days travel and Okiziwakiya, Sun Man and twenty of his best fighting Crow braves, Luzahan, Ciqala and their animal brothers reach the large boulders, which Sun Man described to Okiziwakiya back in his village. They are located just before the narrow cliff area. Okiziwakiya decides to camp there and scout ahead to clear their way to the Jicarilla Apache village. Sun Man makes napeonwoglaka (uses sign language) to Okiziwakiya, asking for Okiziwakiya's wolf brother Šungmanitu Aitancan, to come and join with him, and to leave his pack behind with Okiziwakiya. He explains that he can run fast all day long and so can Šungmanitu Aitancan.

He further explains in sign language, that he will scout what stands between them and their plan to takpe (to come upon, attack) the Jicarilla Apache enemy. Okiziwakiya agrees with Sun Man's silent words he has signed him, and he will stay back and wait in this chosen area of defense, in case the enemy may be coming. They are!

Sun Man and Šungmanitu Ruler are making amazing progress as they run swiftly and silently through the large trees and are just starting to break out of the trees, when Wolf Ruler abruptly pataka (to come to a stop) and so does his mighty human running mate, Sun Man. About a half mile away in a

Sun Man's Rescue Sends a Strong Message

grass covered prairie, is a large number of Jicarilla Apache warriors heading their way at a fast walking pace. Sun Man counts about two hundred or more of the enemy. He and his loyal šungmanitu scout wheel around and race back to warn Okiziwakiya and his brothers of the danger heading toward them. Šungmanitu is very impressed by this Crow scouting with him and even he cannot out run this wimaca.

The two scouts are running hard as they must warn their war party of what they have seen, so they can all make ready for battle and time is a most valuable asset, when making a place of defense, defendable. All the speed they can make is being given to their scouting mission, to make ready for war.

Until our next campfire visit, where we will finish this big battle in another Campfire Story Telling - "The Great Battle on the High Cliff Edge," may Wakantanka Bless You and hold You in His love. Keep Him in your hearts and minds, as He does each and every one of you great 'campfire story readers'.

Lakota Chief Crazy Horse

Chapter 10

The Great Battle on the High Cliff Edge

Axxaashe (sun – Crow dialect) wi (sun – Lakota dialect) Bachhee (man – Crow dialect) wimaca (a man, a male of the human species – Lakota dialect), also known as: "Sun Man" and Šungmanitu (a wolf) Aitancan (the ruler over) have put a good distance between them and the approaching Jicarilla Apache —one of several bands of Apache Indians, currently living in New Mexico— warriors, who are coming to takpe (make an assault) on them, running fast, as only the fastest heton cik'ala (an antelope) can run, as they reach Okiziwakiya's (to cause to heal up) location. A change of battle plans must be made and quickly from attacking to defending their present position. Okiziwakiya and Sun Man, discuss by signing what to do now that their plan of takpe has no meaning.

They must make a takpe from a defensive position, because they are heavily outnumbered. The enemy is coming to them; there can be no surprise attack on them as previously planned. Luzahan (swift) and Ciqala (little one), agree with Okiziwakiya and Sun Man, and decide this is a very good place to defend against this great number of enemy warriors coming against them. The Jicarilla Apache will not expect to be attacked here in this area they have chosen, and will not be on guard for a possible attack from Okiziwakiya's warriors. The Crow (Apsáalooke – children of the large-beaked bird – Siouan language) and Oglala (to scatter one's own) Lakota (the Siouan people) warriors will takpe on them where Jicarilla Apache do not expect an attack. The plan will be to wait until the enemy approaches the large boulders on the enemy side of the narrow cliff face.

Okiziwakiya and his warriors will wait for some of the enemy in the lead to reach the enemies side, (the southside) of the long cliff face and let them enter in between some of the boulders. From a hidden position behind the boulders there, the Oglala Lakota and Crow and other animal warriors will launch a takpe upon them. The wait is long and stressful, but gives them time to make all war plans for defense ready by Okiziwakiya and his army of brothers.

The Great Battle on the High Cliff Edge

The enemy Jicarilla Apache warriors are closing in on them in large groupings and enter between the boulder where Okiziwakiya and his warriors are waiting. Šungmanitu Aitancan and his entire šungmanitu pack attack the lead column of Jicarilla Apache by coming around from behind the boulders, they have been hiding behind. Okiziwakiya, Sun Man with his warriors, Luzahan and Ciqala, rain down arrows and spears, after Wolf Ruler and his wolf pack retreat, from the totally surprised enemy Jicarilla Apache.

At least twenty-five Jicarilla Apache are killed outright and many are injured. The Jicarilla Apache fall back into the woods for cover to plan their next move. Okiziwakiya's warriors all retreat across the narrow cliff face and take-up defensive positions behind the large boulders on their side of the narrow cliff face and are hidden from the view of any Jicarilla Apache warriors.

Soon enough, loud Jicarilla Apache war cries are heard coming from the boulders across the narrow cliff face, as fifty attacking Jicarilla Apache warriors charge onto the narrow cliff and the leading Jicarilla Apache attacker is about ten feet away from where Okiziwakiya is hidden behind his boulder. The Jicarilla Apache attacker is running fast toward him with a tomahawk.

Suddenly, letting out a loud ferocious growl Okiziwakiya's big brother, the massive brown mato hota (a grizzly bear) and Mato Hota Titakuye (the immediate relatives) grizzly brother springs into action. He attacks at full speed, putting his left shoulder near the wall of the cliffside. He begins clearing all the Jicarilla Apache warriors on the narrow cliff face to his right, knocking them off the narrow ledge, as if they were never there. He did all this by charging between them and the cliff wall, giving them no room to avoid his takpe; he swats them off with his massive paws. They never had any time to fight against him with their weapons, with no room to maneuver.

Mato Ḣota Titakuye caught them completely by surprise, he made them to waglihpa (to fall down, i.e. once) off the cliff edge sending them flying two or three at a time, like falling stars with big voices screaming like šunkmanitus (coyotes) all the way to the bottom of the canyon, probably trying to call on some 'Spirit' to save them, which of course never happened.

The scene was filled with the devastating power the great mato ḣota possessed as a great warrior with courage and self-sacrifice and otakuye (brotherhood) to Okiziwakiya. He went through the enemy Jicarilla Apache warriors on the cliff face, with great ease, like swatting away small flies on summer's lazy day, with one exception, they would not be coming back to annoy him again, ever.

When Mato Ḣota Titakuye reached the south end of the narrow cliff edge, he slid to a stop, turned around and began running back across the cliff edge. It was at this time some Jicarilla Apache braves hidden behind boulders, gained some confidence and came out running and shot arrows at him as he retreated across the narrow edge of the cliff. Mato Ḣota Titakuye was hit by three enemy arrows in his huge rump and let out a snarl as he disappeared among his brothers on the other side of the north cliff face.

Okiziwakiya calls on Wakantanka, the Creator, God, for healing power and feels its power flowing through him. He

The Great Battle on the High Cliff Edge

removes the arrows without causing any more pain to Mato Hota Titakuye, now a hero grizzly brother, who's huge rump feels like new to him and now he stands ready, swinging his big paws, grinning beckoning for more fighting of the enemy Jicarilla Apache. He roars saying in bear talk "Come and meet me in battle, I am here, you do not give me pause to fight you."

With many of the enemy Jicarilla Apache warriors killed or wounded and their leader, their chief, killed on the narrow cliff in the second attack, they elect a new leader before renewing any attacks on the Crow and their brothers. The Jicarilla Apache select, as chief, a warrior who is huge among Indians of his day standing well over six and a half feet tall and heavy with all muscle supported by a large heavily boned frame, his large wide shouldered frame is intimidating to those who are smaller. He is known among his tribe to be fearless.

His name is Cougar Man (Ndolkan Homme - Cougar man – Jicarilla Apache dialect). He is a formidable warrior. A giant of a man standing almost seven feet tall and weighing two hundred eighty pounds, all muscle, tendons and sinew. He was in line to be chief of his village, if their leader is ever killed, which has just happened.

Not only is Cougar Man a big and brave Jicarilla Apache warrior, but he is wise in the ways of fighting his enemies and has killed many in his short life of twenty-three iomaka's (the next year - time).

Okiziwakiya and all his warriors are facing a powerful and cunning foe with Cougar Man now leading the remaining Jicarilla Apache enemy warriors as their new chief. Even though this new threat, by the strength in the Jicarilla Apache ranks has taken place by the death of their former chief and their new leader, Chief Cougar Man. This fact is not known to the Crow and Oglala Lakota braves, defending against them.

Okiziwakiya and Sun Man believe the Creator Wakantanka (The Great Spirit, the Creator, God) and Tatanka Ska Son are watching over them, He will not fight the battles for them, but they are blessed in their wakan (sacred, holy) names. Both braves take time alone from the others, a private time to pray for wisdom and power to overcome their enemy in the upcoming battle for their lives and lives of their villagers.

Tatanka Ska Son's Voice is heard by Okiziwakiya and Sun Man, and them alone from the others who are nearby and in each of their own languages. Tatanka Ska Son speaks through His silent Voice from afar, 'Okiziwakiya, I will give you the wisdom that you pray for to My Father, the Creator of all, as you pray upon bended knees'. Tatanka Ska Son is also speaking to Sun Man and His Words are also heard by Okiziwakiya, 'Sun Man, you will receive the strength of a thousand men this day in battle. The only thing for you both to fear is losing your faith in Wakantanka, My Father and Me, His Son and faithful servant, Who speaks to you now. I give you both the gift of many languages and dialects. This knowledge that I give to you this day will enable you to speak to all your warriors and they will understand. I also tell you, you'll be delivered from harm in this upcoming battle'.

Both Okiziwakiya and Sun Man are listening with bowed heads and much reverence in their hearts. It is good to have faith in Wakantanka and Tatanka Ska Son. All is lost without this

The Great Battle on the High Cliff Edge

faith and Okiziwakiya and Sun Man know this to be true and their trust in the Wakan Ones is unshakable.

Chief Cougar Man has come up with a plan of attack and he puts this plan into action. He sends twenty of his fastest running braves back and around this pass, hoping they will find a way to come in behind the enemy Crow warriors.

He will wait for two moons in the sky, in the position he holds deep in the boulders. He has scouts watching the narrow cliff edge, the path leading to their position. He can hold off any attack from this position with his hundred plus warriors. He has put into action a good plan in his mind. He will wait for the rear attack by his warriors and then charge in a frontal attack as many times as needed, with his remaining warriors using shields to block any arrows or spears from his opposing Crow warriors. Chief Cougar Man and his warriors make camp and start a great campfire and begin a preparation dance of war, meant to scare his enemy, as if he had many more warriors and, also to make his braves ready in spirit for the battle to come.

Okiziwakiya sends Šungmanitu Aitancan and his wolf pack back around behind Sun Man's warriors, to scout and watch for any enemy who might try to come in and attack them from behind in a surprise attack. He and Sun Man have been given wisdom by Tatanka Ska Son on how to use their forces.

Two nights later Šungmanitu Aitancan's wolf pack sneak in on the twenty Jicarilla Apache braves while they sleep with no night guards posted on duty. A big mistake as each šungmanitu moves in, before the Jicarilla Apache braves can barely clear their blankets. The wolves attack the Jicarilla Apache braves before they are given any warning of their coming against them.

The big powerful wolves are more than a match for the sleepy warriors caught off guard. When one Jicarilla Apache warrior is killed, the šungmanitu, who is victorious in his individual battle immediately, helps any other šungmanitu brother subdue the enemy Jicarilla Apache warrior he is in single combat with. The fight is over in minutes. Šungmanitu Aitancan has not lost a single brother wolf. Šungmanitu Aitancan Ruler and his brothers, begin the return trip to help Okiziwakiya's warriors, back at their fighting position among the boulders by the northern narrow cliff edge.

When Šungmanitu Aitancan and his wolf pack come back, — some šungmanitu with the marks of battle— Okiziwakiya knows they have been completely successful in battle and prevented an attack from the rear and he is very pleased by their bravery, as is Sun Man, knowing his Crow braves are still uninjured and continuing their mission.

All celebrate Šungmanitu Aitancan (Wolf Ruler) and his šungmanitu brothers, hugging them and giving them some dried tatanka meat and mni (water) to drink and tending some of the wounded, which Okiziwakiya tends to with his healing powers. It is a happy camp the warriors share this night.

Chief Cougar Man has waited for his braves he sent to attack his enemy Crow from the rear, but they have not attacked or returned and he is not going to wait any longer for them to come back. He will attack at first light with his hundred strong warriors, using all his Jicarilla Apache warriors on frontal attack and try to overwhelm them with numbers, with each warrior

The Great Battle on the High Cliff Edge

armed with tomahawks and spears for thrusting at the enemy. His warriors leading the attack will carry burning torches, in case the great bear attacks again. He believes that will defeat any threat to his attacking warriors.

Sun Man ask Okiziwakiya, who both have now been given the ability and knowledge of the Crow Nation, Oglala Lakota Nation, and other languages as needed, from Tatanka Ska Son,

"How are you feeling about our war plans"? Okiziwakiya answers, "Our God has blessed us my dear brother."

The gift of languages has increased their knowledge and ability to communicate with each warrior brother or different tribesman speaking different languages. This makes it much easier to plan their battle against their enemy, good communication skills are always very important to sound planning.

If Sun Man can put his part of the plan he has thought of into action, with Okiziwakiya's agreement, he believes they will be successful in this war's outcome. Okiziwakiya answers, "Wakantanka is with you and your brother Crow braves who, also stand with him."

Sun Man begins putting more of his plan into action, by pushing two very large boulders up just out of sight of the enemy's view. He places each huge boulder, sided by side leaving just enough room between the boulders for a man or horse to pass through.

Everyone is surprised to see this great strength in a human being, all but Okiziwakiya, Luzahan and Ciqala. This unbelievable strength of Sun Man is greater than all of them together and with the help of all of the enemy warriors. All warriors together could not have moved those big boulders like this man given great strength by Wakantanka. Now, with the moving of the big boulders, the enemy still could come through, but only one at a time.

Sun Man asks Okiziwakiya, Luzahan, Ciqala, Mato Hota Titakuye, Šungmanitu Aitancan, along with all his šungmanitu brothers and his own Crow warriors to hide behind other boulders and take on any enemy that might get past him, for he will meet the enemy Jicarilla Apache warriors when they come, holding only his heavy shield and a round heavy stone-headed tomahawk, as his killing weapon.

Sun Man continues telling his plan in Crow dialect and Oglala Lakota dialect of his battle plan, telling all gathered around him, "As I strike them, you each must pull them through past me, do not let them pile up, push them over the cliff near us, so the enemy will think they got through and will continue to attack. If any get past me alive, they must be killed." Okiziwakiya responds saying, "Sun Man, your plan for battle will be done my brother. Your plan is a good plan and I like it. Wakantanka is with your powerful hand and in Him we must all trust." Everyone takes his position behind the cover of boulders and trees and await the Jicarilla Apache attack.

Chief Cougar Man sends his first wave of braves running across the narrow cliff face, side by side in a column of twos and when they reach the other side of the cliff face; he sees and thinks his warriors are getting through.

Later, after many have gone over to the north side of the cliff, Chief Cougar Man leads the full charge of most of the remaining warriors, leaving a small rear guard. He believes he has routed

The Great Battle on the High Cliff Edge

the enemy in fear of his power and leadership, as the new chief of his Jicarilla Apache village. Little does his pride show him now, but soon, he will know the power of Wakantanka through the hand of His Chosen Children, the Oglala Lakota and all other believers, like Sun Man.

Sun Man lets the first two Jicarilla Apache braves through, out of sight of the others and strikes them, one over the head and the other in the chest, with his heavy stone tomahawk and they go down in a limped heap, dropping their fire torches. Each Jicarilla Apache brave that comes through between the boulders is struck by the strong arm of Sun Man, welding his tomahawk with crushing blows. Each enemy is taken by surprise and by the great strength and speed of Wakantanka's Crow warrior and is thrown over the high cliff, down into the deep canyon below.

Chief Cougar Man and his war party of braves begin their natan (to make an attack, to go after and rush upon) on Sun Man. At this same moment the twenty Crow braves, Sun Man sent earlier to go around and attack from the rear on Chief Cougar Man's war party, launch their own attack on the remaining rear-guard Jicarilla Apache braves, killing all but two, who escape.

All the while the battle is raging across the cliff face, as Chief Cougar Man's turn comes to fight Sun Man face to face, he comes through the two boulders charging at Sun Man in a rage, lusting for blood and ready for battle, as he charges through to meet him. Before he can strike with his tomahawk, he is instantly grabbed by the throat by Sun Man, who has been waiting for him to come to attack him. Chief Cougar Man is lifted high in the air and held at arm's length, helpless like a šungmanitu pup held up by his tail and he is easily disarmed of his weapons, as he is violently shaken back and forth trying to breathe, through the fear he is feeling.

Chief Cougar Man is totally helpless to try to fight against the power of Sun Man, as he struggles in vain to regain his footing and breathe again. Sun Man slings Chief Cougar Man back to Okiziwakiya's position and yells, "Okiwinja (to bind down thoroughly) him with leather straps and keep him alive." Six Crow braves easily okiwinja Chief Cougar Man, before he recovers any of his fighting strength. Sun Man continues to fight all the remaining Jicarilla Apache braves and kills them all with his mighty arm and stone tomahawk.

All the dead Jicarilla Apache are thrown over the cliff, as Sun Man directed. This will be a warning to any Jicarilla Apache, who might come looking for Chief Cougar Man and his warriors. They will find their fellow warriors open graves below the high cliff face, a burial mound of sun-bleached bones. A true testament to Wakantanka's power through those He blesses, with special gifts, talents and protection.

Night fall finds all the Crow and Oglala Lakota braves celebrating a great victory, as Mato Hota Titakuye and Šungmanitu Aitancan and his šungmanitu pack eat near a huge campfire. Sun Man breaks away to be by himself and offers up a prayer of thanks to Wakantanka, for blessing him with this great victory.

Chief Cougar Man is untied from his bonds of leather fastenings and brought to the warmth of the campfire by six Crow braves with spears pointed at him and he is given food and water to revive him. He cannot believe he has been freed to eat and offered water, because he is a prisoner of war and should be tortured and killed, as his tribe does with prisoners taken in battle. He is very confused by all that has happened in this one-sided battle, and his terrible defeat as future chief of his Jicarilla

The Great Battle on the High Cliff Edge

Apache tribe, could be in question, if he manages to escape and live.

Tatanka Ska Son appears from the sky in darkness and blue light surrounds Him as He lands near the huge campfire. All bow down or go to their knees in reverence, except for Chief Cougar Man, who is frozen in place by fear and awe. Tatanka Ska Son speaks, "Cougar Man, listen closely, Sun Man has spared you, as I have instructed him to do so before his strong hands held you by your throat. You alone have been spared, although two of your rear-guard warriors have escaped and are returning to your village and will tell a story of your defeat, believing you are dead. They will be surprised to see you alive when you return to them. Now go to your village and Jicarilla Apache people, and teach them of My Father, Wakantanka, and His Son, Me, Tatanka Ska Son. You are to live in peace with all others as brothers.

"You will live respecting Mother Earth as your own mother and love your enemies as your own brothers; for We are all Sons of Wakantanka and will serve Him in this life He has given each one, so they may be with Him in the life after they "walk on" to Mahpiya (Heaven). Do you understand My Words, Cougar Man"?

Chief Cougar Man falls to his knees and answers in the Jicarilla Apache dialect, "I hear Your Words and see Your Power through the mighty warrior before me (speaking of Sun Man). I will do as You say." Upon hearing Chief Cougar Man's answer, Tatanka Ska Son lifts off into the night's darkness.

Everyone stands and looks at Sun Man, as he approaches Chief Cougar Man and gives him food and water and bids him a farewell in an act of friendship. Chief Cougar Man is completely surprised by what has happened to him this day that has changed his life forever in a good way. He will tell this story for the rest of his life as he teaches his people of friendship and love given by Tatanka Ska Son. The peaceful ways of Tatanka Ska Son and the culture of the Oglala Lakota people, who live within the lap of Mother Earth, given to all by Wakantanka.

This is what Chief Cougar Man has witnessed this day and he will take this story back to his village as fast as he can run on his long legs. If he is given the gift of leadership as chief of his tribe, he will lead them in peace and teach them of Tatanka Ska Son by many campfires. Little does Chief Cougar Man know that has been the plan of Wakantanka all along!

Okiziwakiya and his warriors leave for the Crow village, led by Sun Man and his Crow braves. After spending many nights in camp and in travel, they reach the Crow village and bid Sun Man and his Crow braves good bye. Some Crow villagers come out and wave to Okiziwakiya and his strange army of human beings and forest animals. Sun Man has invited them to his village to let his villagers give them the gift of welcome, but Okiziwakiya, Luzahan and Ciqala are anxious to reach their Oglala Lakota village and reunite at their own tiwahe (a household).

They know their families and many more have been worrying about their disappearance and may be looking for them by this time. They must hurry back to the Oglala Lakota village there are many campfire stories to tell.

Until we meet again beside the campfire in book two, <u>Dangerous Missions in the Northwest</u>, when Okiziwakiya gets his new name. Stay strong my dear 'campfire story readers' and friends to Wakantanka and His Son, Tatanka Ska Son. They will Bless You and keep you always; you are never alone in this world with Them at your side.

Other bear names of interest:

1) mato \ma-tó\ (the gray or polar bear)
2) šakehanska - nickname for "waonze"- (the nickname for grizzly bear)
3) hinsko \hín-sko\ (so big, so large) mato hota \ma-tó hò-ta\ (big grizzly bear)
4) waowešica \wa-ó-we-ši-ca\ (a bear, in general)
5) mato cincala \ma-tó ciŋ-cà-la\ (a bear's cub)

Heȟak iktomi

Appendix

ALPHABETICAL BOOK ONE LAKOTA AND OTHER MEANINGS

Most meaning words Lakota dialect came from the Lakota dictionary – Lakota-English/ English-Lakota New Comprehensive Edition; Compiled and Edited by Eugene Buechel and Paul Manhart
University of Nebraska Press, 2002.

a·can·te·šil·ya·kel \a-can-te-šil-ya-kel\ (sadly or sorrowfully for)

a·hin·han \a-hiɳ-haɳ\ (to rain upon, to fall as rain does on things)

a·i·tan·can \a-í-taɳ-caɳ\ (the ruler over)

an·imi·kii \an-imi-kii\ (thunder – Animaikii is a giant mythological thunder-bird common to the northern and western tribes. Thunder is caused by the beating of their immense wings - in Chippewa dialect) – wa·kin·yan \wa-kíɳ-yan\ (thunder, the cause and source of thunder and lightning, once supposed by Dakota to be a great bird).

Anishinaabemowin or Anishináabe languages that belong to the Algonquian language family. They historically lived in the Northeast Woodlands and Subarctic. – Source, 'Wikipedia'

Ani·xshin·áabe \Ani-xshin-áabe\ (is the autonym for a group of culturally related indigenous people residing in what are now Canada and the United States. These also include the Odawa, Saulteaux, Ojibwe (including Mississaugas), Potawatomi, Oji-Cree, and Algonquin people. The Anishinaabe means "original person". The Anixshináabe speak many different dialects, as they have many tribes)

A·pa·che \Ə'-paSH\ (a member of a North American people living chiefly in New Mexico and Arizona. The Apache put up fierce resistance to the European settlers and were, under the leadership of Geronimo, the last American Indian people to be conquered)

Aps·á·a·look·e \Aps-á-a-look-e\ (The Crow in Siouan dialect – meaning – "children of the large-beaked bird")

ari·ka·ra \ari-ka-ra\ (running wolf – Crow dialect)

A·tha·bas·kan \A-tha-bas-kan\ (A family of American Indian languages spoken primarily in western Canada, Alaska, and the Southwest – Some Western Apache use this language)

a·wa·ci \a-wá-ca\ (to dance on anything or in honor of)

a·wa·ši·ca·ho·wa·ya \a-wa-ši-cá-ho-wa-ya\ (to cry out on account of)

axxa·ash·e \axxa-ash-e\ (sun – Crow dialect)

ba·ch·hee \ba-ch-hee\ (man – Crow – dialect)

bag·wun·gi·ji·k \bag-wun-gi-ji-k\ (hole in the sky – Chippewa dialect)

bas·axe \bas-axe\ (turtle – Crow dialect)

bii·lee \bii-lee\ (swan – Crow dialect)

bishee \Bi'Shee\ (buffalo – Crow dialect)

bla·ya \blá-ya\ (level, plain)

bua \bua\ (fish – Crow dialect)

Appendix

can·ška \can-šká\ (red-legged hawk, the large white-breasted hawk, a snake eater)

can·te·ki·ya \can-ṫé-ki-ya\ (to love, to have an interest in or affection for, which prompts one to perform benevolent acts)

can·te·yu·kan \caṇ-ṫé-yu-kan\ (to have heart, to be benevolent)

can·to·gna·gya \caṇ-ṫó-gna-gya\ (in a loving manner)

ca·pa \cá-ṗa\ (beaver)

che·é·te \che-é-te\ (wolf – Crow dialect)

Chip·pe·wa \chip-pe-wa\ (The names Chippewa, Ojibway, Ojibwe, Ojibwa all come from an Algonquin word, which means "puckered", mostly because of the shape of their moccasins and how they appeared. The Ojibway call themselves Anishináabe meaning 'original person', all are people of Canada and the United States of America.)

ci·k'a·la \ċi-k'a-la\ (little, very small) – "When used as one word"

ci·qa·la \ċi·q'a-la\ (little one)

Crow \Crow\ (The Crow, called the Apsáalooke in their own Siouan language, or variants including the Absaroka, are Native Americans, who in historical times lived in the Yellowstone Valley, which extends from present-day Wyoming through Montana and into North Dakota, where it joins the Missouri River)

e·han·na \e-háṇ-na\ (long ago)

gun·ga \ġúṇ-ġa\ (proud, with eyes closed not minding others, haughty)

gun·gaga·ya \ġúŋ-ġa-ġa-ya\ (proudly)

ha·ho ha·ho \ha-hó ha-hó\ (express of joy on receiving something)

han·pa \háŋ-ṗa\ (moccasin)

ha·pa·šlo·ka \ha-ṗá-šlo-ka\ (to pull off skin, to chafe)

ha·yu·za \há-yu-za\ (to skin, take off the skin of anything)

he·ḣa·ka \he-ḣá-ḱa\ (the male elk, so called from its branching horns)

he·ḣak i·kto·mi \he-ḣák i-któ-mi\ (a moose)

he·ton \he-tón\ (horned) cik'ala \cí-k'a-la\ - heton cikala (an antelope)

hin·sko \hín-sḱo\ (so big, so large)

hin·to \hin-to\ (gray horse)

ho·gle·gle·ga \ho-glé-gle-ġa\ (the grass pike, or the rainbow fish)

hom·me \hom-me\ (man – Apache dialect)

hui·ya·kas·kes \huí-ya-ḱas-kes\ (ankle ornaments for Sundance)

h'e·h'e·ya \h'e-h'é-ya\ (slobbering)

i·gla·s·to \i-glá-s-to\ (to be left out, incomplete)

i·glu·wan·ka·tu·ya \i-glú-waŋ-ḱa-ṫu-ya\ (to elevate or raise up one's self, over others, i. e. to be proud)

i·gmu·wa·to·gla \i-gmú-wa-tó-gla\ (mountain lion)

Appendix

i·gni \i-gní\ (to hunt, seek for, to follow after e.g. game)

ii·ch·ii·le \ii-ch-ii-le\ (horse – Crow dialect)

i·o·ma·ka \í-o-ma-ka\ (the year next to, the next year - time)

i·tan·can·ka \i-táŋ-caŋ-ka\ (the chief one, lord and master)

i·tun·psi·ca·la \i-túŋ-psi-ca-la\ (the field mouse)

i·wa·gla·mna \i-wá-gla-mna\ (an extra or fresh horse)

i·wan·gla·ka \i-wáŋ-gla-ka\ (to look to, have regard for one's own)

i·ya·ki·ta \í-ya-ki-ta\ (to have an eye to, keep watch on)

i·ya·š'a·pi \í-ya-š'à-pi\ (an acclamation)

jer·ky \jer-ky\ (smoked dried meat – in English language)

Ji·ca·rill·a A·pa·che \JI-ca-rill-a A-pa-che\ (Jicarilla Apache, one of several loosely organized autonomous bands of the Eastern Apache, refers to members of the Jicarilla Apache Nation currently living in New Mexico and speaking a Southern Atabaskan language)

ka·ga·pa \ka-ġá-pa\ (to cut, spread open by cutting, to lay open)

ka·lu·za \ka-lú-za\ (to flow rapidly, as water)

kan·gi·ha mi·gna·ka \kaŋ-ġí-ha mi-gnà-ka\ (a feather disk, resembling the unhcela kagapi)

kan·htal \káŋ-htal\ (relaxed, with a loss of tension)

ka·psan·psan \ka-psáŋ-psaŋ\ (to dangle, swing back and forth, to sway to and fro, as a limb in the water)

ka·tka \ká-tka\ (briskly)

kes·ton \kes-tón\ (a barbed arrowhead)

ki·can \ki-cáŋ\ (cries out loudly)

ku·ka \ku-ká\ (rotten, spoiled, as meat, tender, worn out, as clothes)

La·ko·ta \La-ko-ta\ (Lakota, Nakota and Dakota are the names of three larger Siouan people living generally in the north-central United States of America)

lu·za·han \lú-za-haŋ\ (swift, to be fast, fast running)

Ma·hpi·ya \ma-ḣpí-ya\ (Heaven, the clouds, the afterlife of mankind)

ma·ka \ma-ká\ (skunk or pole cat)

ma·ko·k'e \ma-kō'-k'e\ (a dug-out, a pit)

mato \ma-tó\ (the gray or polar bear)

ma·to ḣo·ta \ma-tó ḣò-ta\ (the grizzly bear)

ma·tos·kah \ma-tos-kah\ (white bear)

mi·gna·ka \mi-gná-ka\ (to put in under the girdle)

mni \mni\ (water)

na·pe·on·wo·gla·ka \na-ṗé-oŋ-wò-gla-ka\ (sign, signs, signing – to use sign language – to communicate using gestures with hands or other body movement and facial expressions)

na·tan \na-táŋ\ (to make an attack, to go after and rush upon e.g. the enemy)

Appendix

n·dol·kan \n-dol-kan\ (cougar – Apache dialect)

O·gla·la \O-glá-la\ (to scatter one's own – name of one of three larger clans of the Teton Sioux Indian people living in the north-central United States of America)

o·glu \o-glú\ (luck, fortune)

o·ha·mna \o-há-mna\ (smelling of skin – to smell badly)

o·i·pu·ta·ke \o-í-ṗu-ta-k̇e\ (kiss)

o·ki·win·ja \o-kí-wiŋ-ja\ (to bind down thoroughly)

o·ki·yu·ta \ó-k̇i-yu-ṫa\ (to heal up)

okizi·wa·ki·ya \o-ki-zi-wa-ki-ya\ (to cause to heal up)

O·ma·ha \O-ma-ha\ (The Omaha Indian people are from the Upper Missouri River – Omaha in their dialect means – flat water)

on·ši·la \óŋ-ši-la\ (to have mercy on)

o·ta·ku·ye \o-ṫá-k̇u-ye\ (brotherhood, relationship, relations, kinfolk, kinship)

o·wa·mni·o·mni \o-wá-mni-o-mni\ (an eddy, whirl-pool, a cyclone)

o·ya·te \o-yá-ṫe\ (a people, nation, tribe, or band)

pa·e \ṗa-é\ (to inflict punishment in order to prevent future lapses)

pa·ta·ka \ṗa-tá-k̇a\ (to come to a stand as a horse does)

pe·ša \pé-ša\ (the headgear used in the Omaha dance, and made of the porcupine skin, the Omahas being the first to use it)

pe·tu·spe \pe-tú-spe\ (a firebrand with which to start a fire)

po·rt \po-rt\ (left side – English language used in Nautical terms)

port·a·ging \port-a-ging\ (carrying a canoe or boat – French/Canadian dialect)

pte·ha·šla \pte-há-šla\ (a buffalo hide from which the hair has been removed)

pte·he wa·pa·ha \pte-hé wa-pà-ha\ (horned headgear)

pte·o·pta·ye \pte-ó-pta-ye\ (a buffalo herd)

sin·te·han·ska \sin-té-han-ska\ (whitetail deer)

sin·te·sa·pe·la \sin-té-sa-pe-la\ (black-tail deer or mule deer)

Si·oux La·ko·ta \Si-oux La-kó-ta\ (Lakota, Nakota, and Dakota are the names of three of the larger Siouan people living generally in the north-central United States of America)

ska \ska\ (white)

son (son) (a boy or man in relation to either or both of his parents – English language)

stone \stone\ (throw stones at – English language)

Sun·dance \Sun-dance\ (Sundance – English language (Wiwanyank Wacipi – Lakota dialect)

ša·ke·hans·ka \sa-ke-hans-ka\ (nickname for a grizzly bear)

ša·ke·hu·te s'e hin·gle \ša-ké-hu-te s'e hin-gle\ (angry as a bear)

Appendix

ši·ca·ho·wa·wa \ši-cá-ho-wa-wa\ (to cry out)

šun·gblo·ka \šuŋ-gbló-ka\ (the male horse or dog)

šun·gma·ni·tu \šuŋ-gmá-ni-tu\ (a wolf)

šun·gma·ni·tu ai·tan·can \šuŋ-gmá-ni-tu ai-táŋ-can-ka\ (wolf ruler)

šun·gwin·ye·la \šuŋ-gwíŋ-ye-la\ (a mare horse – female horses)

šun·ka·wa·kan \šúŋ-ka-wa-kan\ (a horse)

šun·kma·ni·tu \šuŋ-kmá-ni-tu\ (a coyote)

šun'·onk'onpa \šuŋ-óŋ-k'oŋ-pa\ (pony or dog travois, drag, the original vehicle of the Dakotas displaced by the wagon, the former consisting of two poles, one pair of ends fastened together and placed on the back of the pony or dog with a strap around the breast, the other pair of ends dragging over the ground. The baggage rested on the 'šunktacangleška' baggage basket which is tied across the poles behind the tail of the horse or dog)

ta·ha \ta-há\ (a deerskin)

ta·ha·lo \ta-há-lo\ (a hide)

ta·hu·hu·te \ta-hú-hu-te\ (nape of the neck)

ta·ḣca \tá-ḣca\ (deer – venison)

ta·kan \ta-káŋ\ (sinew taken from the back of a deer, buffalo, or cow which is used for thread)

ta·ko·da \ta-ko-da\ (friend to everyone)

ta·ko·laku \ta-kó-laka\ (his special friend)

ta·kpe \ta-kṗé\ (to come upon, attack; make an attack)

ta·ku·ya \ta·kú-ya\ (to have one for a relation)

tan·ka \táŋ-ka\ (large, great in any way)

tan·ni·ka \taŋ-ní-kȧ\ (old, worn out, ancient, archaic)

ta·tan·ka \ta-táŋ-k̇a\ (a male buffalo)

ta·tan·ka ska \ta-táŋ-k̇a ska\ (white buffalo)

Ta·tan·ka Ska Son \Ta-táŋ-k̇a Ska Son\ (a male buffalo, white, a man – Son of God Tatanka Ska Son – Jesus Christ Son of God, in the form of a white buffalo)

ta·wa·kpe ya \ta-wa-kpe ya\ (to go to attacking)

Te·ton \Te-ton\ (another term for Lakota)

Te·ton Si·oux \Te-ton Si-oux\ (name of the Lakota people and the Nakota and Dakota bands)

ti·pi \tí-ṗi\ (teepee or tent or lodge)

ti·ta·ku·ye \tí-ta-k̇u-ye\ (the immediate relatives)

ti·wa·he \ti-wá-he\ (a household, i.e. including persons as well as things)

to·ka \tó-k̇a\ (one of a foreign or hostile nation, an enemy)

to·ka·ta \to-k̇á-ṫa\ (in the future, or the future)

to·la·hca·ka \tō'-la-ḣca· k̇a\ (very blue)

to·ma·hawk \to-ma-hawk\ (the tomahawk originated from the Algonquin Indians of the Sioux Nation. The word came from the

Appendix

words tamahak or tamahakan. The Native American Indians regularly used tomahawks made from stone heads which were attached to wooden handles and tied with strips of rawhide or leather. Some used sharp stone heads for chopping and cutting, also as weapons. Some tomahawks used a heavy rounded stone head for fighting instead of sharp stone heads.)

to·wa·on·ši·la \tó-wa-oṇ-ši-la\ (his mercy)

tra·vois \tra-vois\ (a type of sled formerly used by North American Indians to carry goods, consisting of two joined poles dragged by a horse or dog – see šunónkonpa)

tu·šu·he·yun·pi \tu-šú-he-yuṇ-pi\ (a travois, a drag, i.e. tent or tipi poles tied together to pack things on)

un·hce·la ka·ga·pi \uṇ-hcé-la kà-ġa-pi\ (the feather disk attached to the back of a dancer, so called because of the central part appears like a cactus; a dance bustle)

wa·chi·wi \wa-chi-wi\ (dancing girl)

wa·cin·hin \wá-ciṇ-hiṇ\ (the headdress of a Dakota man, anything standing up on the head, e.g. feathers, down or soft feathers, etc.)

wa·cin·hin sa·psa·pa \wá-ciṇ-hiṇ sa-psà-pa\ (black plumes)

wa·cin·hin·ya \wá-ciṇ-hiṇ-ya\ (to use for a plume)

wa·ci·pi \wa-cí-pi\ (dancing, a dance)

waglih·pa \wagli-pa\ (to fall down, i.e. once)

wa·hin·kpe \wa-híṇ-kpe\ (arrow)

wa·htin·yan \wa-htíṇ-yaṇ\ (to be fond of, to care for or about, to love, as in expressing love of any members of the family)

wa·kan \wa-káŋ\ (sacred, holy, consecrated, incomprehensible, special, possessing or capable of giving)

wa·kan'·e·con·pi·la \wa-káŋ-e-coŋ-pi-la\ (magic, tricks of jugglery)

Wa·kan·tan·ka \Wa-káŋ-taŋ-ka\ (the Great Spirit, The Creator, God)

wa·kan wa·ci·pi \wa-káŋ wa-cì-pi\ (a sacred dance)

wa·kan·yan \wa-káŋ-yaŋ\ (in a sacred, holy, or wonderful, or even a mysterious way)

wa·kin·yan \wa-kíŋ-yaŋ\ (the thunderbird, so titled for the natural world of space the bird shares with thunder and lightning)

wa·ki·ta \wá-ki-ta\ (to look out for, to watch)

wa·le·ga \wa-lé-ġa\ (the bladder)

wa·le·ga mi·ni·ya·ye \wa-lé-ġa min-i-ya-ye\ (a water jug)

wa·na·gi·ya·ta \wa-ná-ġi-ya-ta\ (in the land of spirits)

wan·bli·gle·ška \wan-bli-gle-ška\ (spotted eagle)

wan·hi \waŋ-hí\ (flint – a hard rock used to make sparks, by striking it against another flint rock and used to start a fire or make arrow heads and spear heads)

Wa·ni·ki·ye \Wa-ní-ki-ye\ (the Savior, i.e. Jesus Christ of Nazareth in Israel)

wa·ni·ye·tu \wa-ní-ye-tu\ (winter; a year)

wan·ju \wáŋ-ju\ (an arrow pouch – in Lakota dialect, i.e. a 'quiver' in English language)

Appendix

wan·tan·ye·ya \waŋ-tán-ye-ya\ (be skillful in shooting)

wa·o·we·ši·ca \wa-ó-we-ši-ca\ (a bear, in general)

wa·pa·ha he·ton·pi \wa-pá-ha he-tòn-pi\ (a horned headdress)

wa·pe·to·ke·ca \wá-ṗe-to-ḱe-ca\ (a sign, a mark, a boundary)

wa·ši·cun \wa-ší-cuŋ\ (the white man, as used disparagingly)

wa·to·gya \wató-gya\ (to spoil, ruin; to take vengeance, retaliate, to kill)

wa·wa·kan·kan \wa-wá-kaŋ-kaŋ\ (one who does wonderful things)

wa·wa·ša·gya \wa-wá-ša-gya\ (to render worthless)

wa·ya·hlo·ka \wa-yá-ḣlo-ka\ (to persuade, make an impression talking)

wa·ya·ka \wa-yá-ḱa\ (a captive taken in war, a prisoner)

wi \wi\ (the sun or the moon; a month; a personification of the most immense power in creation, for it determines all seasons)

wi·ca·ša \wi-cá-ša\ (man, a man, mankind)

wi·ca·t'e \wí-ca-t'e\ (an instrument with which to kill – Lakota dialect – hatchet or club – English language)

wi·hi·ya·la \wí-hi-ya-la\ (the passing sun, the measure of clock time, the hour of the day)

wi·ma·ca \wi-ma-ca\ (a man, a male of the human species)

wi·no·na \wi-no-na\ (first born daughter)

wi·sma·hin \wi-smá-hiŋ\ (an arrowhead)

Wi·wan·yank Wa·ci·pi \Wi-wáŋ-yank Wa-cì-ṗi\ (the Sundance, a Dakota and Lakota tribal celebration of endurance in behalf of relatives or friends)

wi·ya·ta·pi·ka wacipi \wi-yá-ta ṗi-k̇a wa-cí-ṗi\ (a single women's dance, one performed by single young women only, and two young men do the drumming and singing)

wi·yo·hi·yan·pa \wi-yó-hi-yaŋ-ṗa\ (the east, rising sun)

wo·hle·pe s'e \wo-ḣlé-ṗe s'e\ (standing upright)

wo·on·ši·la \wó-oŋ-ši-la\ (mercy)

wo·wi·tan·wa·ya \wō'-wi-ṫan·wa·ya\ (to glory in)

yu·a·ja·ja \yu-á-ja-ja\ (to explain, to make clear e.g. a doctrine)

yu·go \yu-ġó\ (to be fatigued)

yu·o·ni·han \yu-ó-ni-haŋ\ (to honor, treat with attention)

yu·o·ni·han·yan \yu-ō'-ni-haŋ-yaŋ\ (honoring, treating politely)

yu·tke·ya \yu-tk̇é-ya\ (deeply, as said of a bluff shore where the water is deep)

zon·ta \zóŋ-ṫa\ (honest, trustworthy)

zu·ya \zu-yá\ (to go out with a war party, to lead out a war party)

Made in the USA
Columbia, SC
13 December 2022